THE GREEDY BARBARIAN

A NOVEL

BY

KAKWENZA RUKIRABASHAIJA

theworldiswatching

First Published in 2020 by Kisana Consults
Second Published in 2022 by Kitara Nation
Third Published in 2022 by theworldiswatching

Cover Illustration by: Chris Atukwasize Ogon
Layout by: Doris Kyakyo

Published by theworldiswatching
Produced by BoD - Books on Demand, Norderstedt

ISBN (print version): 978-3-9825132-0-1
ISBN (e-book): 978-3-9825132-1-8

FOREWORD

It is very rare that novels leap out of their cosseted literary circles to ignite political firestorms. In the last three decades we may struggle to count a handful, but you will be hard-pressed to recollect much beyond Salman Rushdie's *The Satanic Verses.*

So when the news first came in 2020 that Kakwenza Rukirabashaija had been arrested, and then tortured for his novel, the general reaction was befuddlement. Tortured for fiction? Had someone with too many unused handcuffs and electric chairs lost their sense of humor? But sense of humor and torture racks? The question was how to digest the news that a novel was now a threat to state security.

The initial shock passed, and then the frenzied search for the book began. And when you managed to get a copy, there it was, all 140 pages of it, a slim, innocent volume no heavier than a packet of cigarettes. The most iconic, outward feature of it was the cartoonishly basic cover illustration. There was little on the frontispiece beyond the requisite, and when the body of text started, there was the abruptness with which it just happened; no fanfare corresponding to the hurricane it had kicked off. You hesitated to begin reading, for the words themselves were already supercharged by the madness swirling around them. And then you started reading.

And there it was, a mild-mannered, evocative description of the pastoral, a narrative told at a certain level, assured pace, not lagging behind the reading pace, not charging away from it with too many commas and semicolons.

We meet Ingabire and straightaway take to her. We meet her husband, Rukundakanuzire and their marriage has some of the elegiac, passionate tenderness that often make the pastoral appealing. The humor is bucolic, coarse, unrepentant jokes. When the author seats us out in the night on one of Rukundakanuzire's nocturnal peregrinations as he sits...

> ....recuperating from the bites, he heard shrill cries emanating from the house. He had put off going back home because of tobacco and mulling over whether to restart his long-forgotten tradition of night dancing or abandon it for good...

...we take to him already. We know these stories; we know the kind of man who sits recklessly on a termite mound. But it's the bites, and the places where the bites are inflicted that provokes the first belly laugh.

So the question; what was all the state goon ire about? Perhaps they did not like his grammar? Or was the diction damaging to national development? Or had the Ugandan goons discovered that terrorists were now turning to novel-writing?

You read on, and as these things go, in the history of books that frightened absolutist powers, *The Greedy Barbarian,* like its forebears, struck you by a certain degree of plainness. They are always plain books, even clumsy in parts, the prose direct and unadorned, as though the authors were deliberately toning down, dimming their

own lights in a kind of reverse aesthetic.
They must all be mad, is the conclusion you reach.

Except that, as with a book like this, you needed a key to unlock it, and even right from the beginning, there is a literary puzzle to work out:
The Greedy Barbarian is a novel a Ugandan would instantly understand, for the author has reached out to an ancient, pre-colonial literary form to write this book. In times past, stories abounded in Uganda of men and women neither human nor gods who might attempt to be heroic but did not fully escape villainy. A Ugandan school child will know the outlines of such tales as of beads and spears that tore brothers apart, of a prized bull sinking traceless into the earth and taking in tow, the fortunes of an entire people, the stories of a rainbow escalator that leads the graces of heaven into the evil of earth and deeper, and of such names as Isaza, Kintu, Nyinamwiru, Gipir, Ndahura, Walumbe.

Kakwenza has eschewed modern literary fads to adopt that unadorned clarity of classical tales. This book is a latter-day retelling of a Ugandan foundational myth. Like the tales of yore, there is here a great helping of magical realism, which is deployed as plot device, as when changing into a lion or snake saves the main character, so that in this book, as in tales past, we not only have half-god, half-men creatures, but also men as half-beasts; fantastic shape shifters, changelings who popped in and out of existence. And what of the shadowy Chwezi cult in both the novel and the myths?

Could this be the key to understanding the furore over the novel? Is the cult, along with Rukundakanuzire's predilections, still alive and its adherents have no sense of humor? Kakwenza posts a question - and this question being the structural spine of the story: suppose something went wrong in the transfiguration from half-beast to full man, and rather than become man, the beast popped into this world raw?

And so we meet Kayibanda. In his ancestry, there are the ingredients already for something to go very wrong. There is his grandfather Rukundakanuzire with a very unpleasant, dark secret. Then, there is the manner of his conception, which is the reverse of immaculate, for which the author kindly spares us the horror of knowing who his actual father is.

Suffice to say that the author is kind enough - or did he lose the will - to not let the story continue anymore in the land of Kayibanda's birth. Bekunda, his mother, who only managed to keep him because she escaped worse, at the hands of her own brothers, ran away to another land.

A new land welcomes Rukundakanuzire's runaway charges. Kagurutsi, who is only one of two kind men in a tale wanting for kindness, in his magnanimity, symbolises the light of the new land. By now, the book has become Kayibanda's story. Kayibanda, right from childhood, is a very ugly literary creature, a one-dimensional monstrosity more reptilian than human.

We become aware of the magnitude of Kakwenza's narrative; we almost sit up at the realisation that this is a psychoanalytic book, a forensic attempt at asking what goes into the making of monsters.

The Greedy Barbarian goes into that dystopia that few writers dare to imagine, nor summon up the will to keep pursuing right down to its horrifying conclusion. To write like this is to spend a great deal of time staring into the abyss that too often afflicts human society. To read such a tale, is to be drawn into a world with little saving grace, a world of mangled and deformed souls of men and women born of deformity, who have neither the will nor the ability to see beyond that deformity; it is to ask that the reader cast aside expectations that the *summum bonum* of life is progressive moral improvement.

The real question therefore, is not if such men as the central character of this little novel - Kayibanda - happen, but why they do. And what better a medium than a novel to excavate beneath a life of depravity to investigate why Kayibanda happened? Keyed to this possibility, Kakwenza goes at the question (the why) with some keenness at detail. He begins from the pre-beginning. And given that men of Kayibanda's ilk evoke the greatness of their ancestry to justify their actions, Kakwenza follows that trail to find, not spleandour, but the mother load of depravity.

From there, the author suggests, nothing can go right. Could it be the spirits of darkness that commanded the paterfamilias of Kayibanda's family to walk the night and eat the forbidden? Is that what denies the narrative arches of these characters to find redemption? Why can they not find fulfillment? Why is heroism ever so elusive? This is the story of characters who are neither happy nor good. Mirth and goodwill barely show up but are sucked away. In the moral universe that birthed Kayibanda's sensibility (if such a thing becomes him), what approximates good is bodily beauty, a pagan cult of the flesh. There is no inner beauty, and as with such cults, beauty brings, not redemption but the evil eye of fate. Neither god nor man (once separated) are good nor trustworthy.

What becomes of men whose gods set no punitive laws but side with whoever does what they wish? What became of their moral compass if they ever had one? By the time we begin to ask such questions, we are already on the moral skids already, and not halfway into the book, the one man with a good heart, Kagurutsi, who saved Kayibanda and his mother, sums up Kayibanda when he says...

> My son, you have become a disaster in the whole village, school and community. Yet at home you give the impression of being a good boy. You are a hypocrite with a very bad demeanour...

This "demeanour", as understatedly as it is put by the one person who loved Kayibanda without needing to, of whom we wonder why not a smidgeon of goodness rubbed off from, will stretch into its fullest length, and we watch as willing after naive men and women come into Kayibanda's universe only to regret it. But do we have the wherewithal to cope with what this greedy barbarian will become?

Kakwenza would have needed dollops of his comedic sense to endure what it takes to see through a book like this. But a sense of humor in a writer is always an unsubtle warning sign of darkness; if we laughed too loudly at how the novel opens, we know it when the loan of humor is recalled with a steep interest, for we have before us the full display of a man's character, his inability to be loyal, his inherited night-dancing and perversions that make this character unfit even for this world.

It is a book for which Kawkenza has paid a very steep price from those who failed to see the funny side of the story. It is often said in some parts of Africa that when you raise a stick for whatever reason, it is the guilty dog that will bolt, and if any powers felt grazed by a tale, it was only an affirmation that those half-men, half-beasts of ancient tales, still live with us, for in their catastrophic failure of humor, they outdid the worst aspects of the tale.

A.K. Kaiza, 2022

This book is a work of fiction. Names, characters, places and incidents either are products of the author's imagination or are used fictitiously. Any resemblance to actual events or locales or persons, living or dead, is entirely coincidental and beyond the intent of the author.

Part One

Ingabire was in the kitchen preparing *emikaro* for her husband who had gone to tend the cattle. When she had finished putting the thick concoction in the *rwaabya*, she pushed it under the wooden rack with her arm and crouched over the peelings towards the stool where the candle stood. She energetically blew into the flame to extinguish the light, and nipped the hot wax to stop the foul smell. She gathered herself up and sauntered out of the kitchen through the door, the only opening in the round grass-thatched mud-and-wattle structure. She had been home alone. Rukundakanuzire had married her not long ago.

It was at dusk. The sun had sunk behind the hills already. She was lonely and scared because her husband had not come back home yet the day was losing the battle to the impatient night. She darted hither and thither and suddenly remembered that she had not yet fetched water.

'When shall I have a child so that I can stop going to fetch water aaahhh?' she murmured to herself.

She briskly walked to the house and picked up a round twenty-litre jerrican. She rushed down to the well through a forest of coffee and many shrubs. She was quite tall and, for a while, she had to duck in order to avoid the lower boughs of the trees and walked while bent over until she got through the forest.

When she reached the well, she squatted to sink the jerrican into the calm, silent water. A scared frog jumped between her open legs and sought refuge in her skirts. She jumped up and the jerrican slipped from her hands, going to freely float on the water. The frog lost its grip, perhaps because Ingabire had jumped and shaken her skirts vigorously. It dropped down onto the marshy ground and, in another jump, dived back into the well. Her heart pounding and her breath heavy, Ingabire cursed the impertinent frog and sauntered away to look for a stick to drag the jerrican back from the farthest corner of the well where the waves had pushed it.

A stone's throw away from home, the smell of tobacco that pervaded the entire surroundings was a clear signal that Rukundakanuzire was already home. They loved each other, save for the fact that he was impatient to receive good news from Ingabire that she was expecting another member of the family - a baby. It had been two months since she had married Rukundakanuzire.

His father Rwabutwiigi had been forced to cough up thirty cows and ten sheep as bride price to Ingabire's father before he could marry his beautiful daughter. His father had not negotiated because

Rukundakanuzire was his beloved and only son. In any case, he had the cows, so he thought it useless and mean to negotiate over a mere thirty cows and ten sheep. Instead, he gave out twenty more. One evening, when he was driving the cattle with his son, Rwabutwiigi showed his son part of the hill where he wanted him to establish his homestead. It was on a plateau and two hills away from home. The slopes of the hill were dotted with coffee trees and banana plantations, and the valley was verdant with swamp and sources of water.

Rukundakanuzire felt very discomfited because he had nowhere to start from. He had just got married and they had barely settled in his hut that stood askew opposite his father's house. Now he was to start afresh, building a house, kitchen, a kraal for the animals, and a cowshed for the calves. The only thing he did not worry about was a latrine, because there was enough bush. He worked tirelessly - and in one month he had set up a home. He had exchanged some cows he had received from his father for labour. Two months later, he and Ingabire were independent.

Rukundakanuzire always got up in the morning and milked the cows. Ingabire would be woken up by the sound of sharp arrows of milk gushing into the bottom of the metallic milk bucket at different intervals. Arising, she would sweep off the litter from the compound and prepare a meal for her husband. The husband spent his days away from home, tending the cows and sheep, and returned home at dusk, when the day was battling with the night.

Ingabire was a beautiful woman who smiled all the time. The dimples that formed in both cheeks whenever she smiled strongly accentuated her angelic beauty. She was incomparably beautiful, and she knew it. Everyone was aware of this, and many were jealous of her. She had well-spaced, snow-white teeth and black gums that held them firmly in place. Ingabire's constant smile seemed to reaffirm her confidence in the beauty of her flawless teeth, or to show off what she had that others lacked. She was such a darling to everyone, which often made Rukundakanuzire insecure, for he was the direct opposite of his wife's beauty. He had long teeth, and the front upper ones poked out between his lips. Even when he was eating, the teeth would not retract. That was how he was born. He had shimmering lush hair though - natural, black and soft - crowning his head, and he would comb it with care and devotion before leaving home to herd the animals. He was very tall and slender, with a sharp-pointed long nose and large ears.

When Ingabire had finished preparing breakfast, she rushed to the house and picked up a spade and went under the tree where she had heaped rubbish. She scooped it several times into the *gutiya,* and the rubbish occupied half of it. She twisted the empty top of the *gutiya* into a sort of rope and tied it.

The rays of the morning sun fell on her but they were ineffectual. She wondered why she was feeling very cold, unlike the previous days when she would wake up without a sweater or *lesu* around her and still not feel cold. Now she felt like wanting more sun; she was feeling very cold and dizzy. Then nausea followed. Spittle flowed from her mouth uncontrollably, she needed her spittoon. As she made two strides to fetch her spittoon from the house, the nausea increased. Suddenly lumps of vomit fell from her mouth to the ground, some splashing on to her feet and clothing. She smelt foul.

Rukundakanuzire had been walking around the compound holding a pail full of milk when he noticed that his wife was not well. He rushed behind the house, where he plucked off bitter leaves from a tree and squeezed them into a cup, making a juice. He forced Ingabire to drink it. She drank it all in five gulps, and suddenly she stopped throwing up. He helped her move into the house where he left her resting prostrate on the bed. At first, she wondered what was wrong with her. Then suddenly she remembered that she had spent four months without having her flow. I'm pregnant! she muttered to herself. She smiled and looked askance at her husband, and then told him the good news.

When Rukundakanuzire had finished separating the calves from the cows, he closed the kraal and the cowshed. He stood on an anthill and looked through the dusk at the verdant valley nestled below the hill. He felt for his breast pocket and took out his pipe, filled it with tobacco, lit a match, touched it to the tobacco and pulled at the pipe. He pulled several times until the desired wreath of smoke surged from his mouth and nose. He smoked until the night was impenetrably dark. He got up and started to move back home, situated several yards away from the kraal. Ever since he had got married, he had restrained himself very hard from night dancing. Rukundakanuzire had inherited the vice from his father Rwabutwiigi, while his father had inherited it from his mother Keihangwe!

He had always asked himself the purpose of stealthily waking up at night, naked, and scurrying around people's homes like a mouse while uttering incantations like he was crazy but found no answer. He had several times vowed to give up the habit but he seemed to be a man whose memory seemed to be like mist. He was encapsulated in a tradition whose origin and comeuppance he was ignorant about. Yet he had promised to resume practising the tradition after some months of marriage. He didn't know how to extricate himself from such a mysterious thing.

Rukundakanuzire pulled on the pipe again and puffed out a funnel-shaped cloud of smoke. He dropped his gaze and realised that while he had been lost in thought, he got down from the anthill and was now standing among a procession of red ants. He leaped up and threw away the pipe. He belatedly realise that the stubborn ants had climbed up his legs and when he jumped upon noticing them, they started stinging him voraciously - from the thighs to the scrotum and the buttocks. He hastily unbuckled his trousers and they crumpled to the ground. Panicking, he stepped out of them with indescribable rapidity and stood wiping the ants away from his body. He cursed under his breath and vowed to burn them the following day.

While he was recuperating from the bites, he heard shrill cries emanating from the house. He had put off going back home, because of tobacco and mulling over whether to restart his long-forgotten tradition of night dancing or abandon it for good. However, he came back to his senses before he could reach a final conclusion.

Ingabire had pushed out a bouncing baby girl, with the help of her mother-in-law. Rukundakanuzire had suggested that she should come and stay with them for a while since she was knowledgeable on antenatal and maternity issues. She was the only one in the village who used to help young women to give birth. She had invaluable experience.

The girl was named Bekunda. She was dark in complexion, and it could already be seen that she would undoubtedly turn out to be as beautiful as her mother. Rukundakanuzire was very happy that his family had increased by one more person; they were three now. But deep down he wondered why she had not produced a boy. He was about to ask but the question disappeared before getting out of his mouth. After a week, Mrs Rwabutwiigi went back to her home. She left when Ingabire had recovered enough from the aftereffects of childbirth to now be able to do house chores and easily attend to Bekunda.

When they were asleep one night, the spirits came through a dream and commanded Rukundakanuzire to get out of the house and engage in night dancing. They warned him that if he did not abide by what culture demanded of him, they would kill Bekunda. He got out of bed, sleepily shuffled towards the door and opened it. The night was very dark outside and he could not see what was beside him and where he was going. He could have easily hit the tree in front of the house after he got out but the spirits guided him, through the village paths and into the forest after several homesteads and two villages. The spirits were in charge of his body; he was moving according to their plan. His soul was sound asleep.

The baby woke up and emitted a loud, shrill cry. The noise woke Ingabire up from deep sleep and she offered the baby her breast to suckle. After a few minutes, she realised that only the baby was with her on the bed! Her man was nowhere to be seen! After asking herself several times where Rukundakanuzire could be, she remembered that he frequently woke up to check on the cows. Sleep caught up with her again and she passed out with Bekunda still suckling ravenously with her toothless gums. Ingabire was woken up at dawn by the howling of the dogs within the neighbourhood.

The sun rays fell on Rukundakanuzire's nakedness. He turned instinctively. He realised that one side of his body was burnt. He turned again and a jutting stone dug into his ribs. He leaped up. He did not understand where he was and how he got there. He passed his hands over his face as if to rub off the unconsciousness but still he did not understand what was going on. He pinched his tummy and felt pain. He understood now that he was somewhere in the bush, lost. But who brought me here and how did I come here? Where are my clothes? he asked himself. He scratched his head in an attempt to remember whatever transpired. He looked at the beautiful morning sun and became aware that the day was still young. He was confused. He cursed. He remembered the weeks before and the escapades he had got enmeshed in, the arguments between him and the inherited traditions imposed on him by his father. He was dumbstruck. How am I going back home naked like this? He did not know the answer. He stood there motionless and speechless, like an effigy.

At dawn, the cow's udders itched; they wanted to be milked. The calves wanted to suckle, too. The mooing from the cows and the calves was deafening. The din from the kraal was boisterous, without any order and formula. Ingabire was worried about her husband. Rivers of tears had started flowing down her cheeks and the sobs that escaped from her throat were uncontrollable. Bekunda, too, was crying incessantly.

Between sobs, Ingabire sang lullabies to the baby to placate her back to sleep, but at first her effort was futile. Finally the baby fell asleep and Ingabire went to the kraal. She opened the cowshed for the calves to suckle. The cows received their calves with excitement, and soon they stopped mooing. The baby slept on peacefully.

She hurried back home and cooked breakfast, but had no appetite for anything. She sat at the threshold of the kitchen and waited for her husband in vain. The cattle started mooing again. This time, the din was worsened by the bleating of the sheep. They were hungry. They had chewed all the cud in their stomachs and they now wanted more grass. Feeling annoyed, she got up and marched to the kraal. She opened it for the cows to get out. Once out, the cows started munching the grass in utmost hunger.

Rukundakanuzire vowed not to go back home in his state of nakedness. He murmured that he would rather wait until nightfall and then he sneaks back home while covered in tree branches so that no one could recognise him. He knew that if he walked through the village on his way back home during the day, he would become the subject of gossip and a laughing stock.

He was hungry though. While climbing up a tree to look for something to cure his hunger, his head hit a wasp nest and the angry insects descended on him, stinging him unsparingly. He shrieked with pain but who was there to help him? Only chirping birds, fluttering butterflies and perhaps some monkeys in the nearby trees. His face swollen, he almost couldn't see. His eyes had sunk into his swollen head and his face had become round like that of a Korean.

Finally, the sun disappeared behind the mountains and he started trekking in the twilight. He walked along the paths and would jump into the bush at the sound of anything he suspected to be human. By the time he got close to his home, he had jumped in and out of bushes innumerable times, earning pierces and scratches at each. The first thing he did was to check on the cattle. He found them well, some chewing the cud while others just stood around in the darkness. Then he sneaked into the house. Fortunately, Ingabire was dead asleep, while the baby was busy breastfeeding. He crouched over them and slept against the wall. The following morning, he refused to reveal his ordeal and internally vowed to die with his secrets.

Bekunda grew up into a beautiful girl and, undoubtedly, she was the favourite child in the whole family. She looked more like her mother in her youth. Rukundakanuzire and Ingabire produced more children, six in number. Being a herdsman, Rukundakanuzire always put emphasis on increasing the number of his cattle. He had inherited the love for cattle from his father.

When Rukundakanuzire married, his father gave them eighty cows and forty sheep as a start. The livestock multiplied and after fifteen years he had close to five hundred head of cattle and eight hundred sheep. He had more animals than his father and everyone else in his village and the four neighboring villages. He became more and more prosperous while his counterparts were mired in poverty. While Rukundakanuzire concentrated on tending his animals with his sons, Ingabire tended to the coffee and food crops with the help of Bekunda. Everyone in the village admired Bekunda. Every man in the village - and in other villages too - wanted to marry Bekunda but Rukundakanuzire vowed to slaughter whichever man he found lurking in the neighbourhood of his home. He constantly told his sons to defend their sister whenever he was away, and he equipped them with fighting skills and weapons like spears and arrows. Everyone feared him because of his incessant warnings.

One day, when Bekunda had turned sixteen, five men from Banya village, which is four villages away from Buregyeya village in the south, came to visit Rukundakanuzire. He was not home when they arrived. However, when they were told that he was not home, they said they would wait for him. They found Ingabire and Bekunda home, preparing dinner. As Bekunda knelt and bent behind the grinding stone, grinding millet, her mother was busy preparing *emikaro*. They busied themselves in the kitchen while the visitors sat in silence on the bench outside in the compound under the mango tree. Bekunda served the four old men *amacunda* in *ebyaanzi* and they thanked her in unison.

"Who are you and what do you want in my home?" Rukundakanuzire, who had appeared unnoticed at the corner of the house facing the old men, said rather rudely.

The four men were all gripped by fright as a result of his sudden appearance and his unwelcoming attitude.

They stood up and bowed their heads in respect to Rukundakanuzire. The one with a shiny, bald head spoke for them all.

"I am Bwengye and I have come here to your home uninvited with my fellow elders from Banya village across the river," he introduced them all. He checked his voice and went on: "We are here because of your daughter Bekunda... Our son Baryabusha wants to marry her. We have fifty cows." Bwengye concluded calmly like a rat negotiating with a cat on what to have for dinner.

Rukundakanuzire opened his eyes wide, so that they almost popped out of their sockets. Without uttering a word, he removed his spear from his shoulder and firmly held it in his right hand, aiming at his target. By the time the old men realised that they were in trouble, Rukundakanuzire had pierced Bwengye in the stomach. He hurriedly reached for the stone on the ground. While he was swinging it to hit one other man on the head, the three unhurt men scattered and disappeared into the coffee plantation. Bekunda and Ingabire were struck by Rukundakanuzire's heinous action. They stood in the kitchen doorway like two logs, motionless and awestruck. Their eyes and mouths were open. Bwengye was writhing on the lawn like a headless snake. A fountain of blood squirted up from his stomach and splashed back onto the helpless body and some onto the grass. Several times, he threw his arms up in the air. Then he finally died.

Rukundakanuzire rushed over, picked up Bwengye's body with energy and rapidity like a vulture and disappeared with it into the coffee plantation.

When Bwengye's family learnt about what had happened to him, they vowed to avenge the brutality that Rukundakanuzire had visited on their family head. On his part, Rukundakanuzire counter-vowed to crush anyone caught tresspassing on his land. Bwengye's family demanded for Bwengye's body but he lied to them that after he had struck him, Bwengye had run away with the others whom he had come with. They searched for the body everywhere but they couldn't find it.

After a year, Baryabusha, Bwengye's son, thought about revenge since his family did not know whether Bwengye had died or not.

"If he died, where is his body? Was he buried?" he asked his mother and brothers. "If he survived, why is he not coming back home?" he added.

They all looked at him miserably, without any answer. Baryabusha collected a sack of peelings and diluted poison in water and poured in the sack. He stuck the remaining peelings in the pocket of his jacket. He hoisted the sack on top of his shoulder and disappeared into the darkness. He trudged towards Buregyeya village to the north.

****

Rukundakanuzire and Ingabire received yet another member of the family - a girl. Now they had five boys and two girls. They were very happy to receive another girl. They named her Umwiza. Bekunda was seventeen when Umwiza was born, and the baby looked a great deal like Bekunda. Bekunda was happy because she had got a sister after living for so long with only brothers. Rukundakanuzire had resumed stealthily getting up at night and going out to night-dance. This time, he would sneak out on his own volition, without being influenced by spirits, and return at cockcrow. Ingabire knew about what was going on but chose to keep quiet.

On the night after Bwengye was murdered and Rukundakanuzire had disappeared with the corpse into the coffee trees, he had woken up and sneaked out of the house like a cat. Ingabire had pretended to be dead asleep but as soon as he got outside the house, she had followed him up to the coffee plantation. She saw him pick up Bwengye's corpse and struggle to carry it on his head. Off he lumbered to the valley, where he met his fellow night dancers. They tore the corpse into pieces with their fingers, putting morsels from it in their mouths and munching away greedily. Several other days he had moved out at midnight and she had followed him, all the way down to the valley, and she had seen him with other men in the trade eat a corpse. She did not want to ask. She would not dare ask, because she knew she would be killed and eaten too.

****

Rukundakanuzire woke up and called out to his sons. He wanted them to accompany him to the kraal to milk the cows. It was six in the morning, and the air was murky. Each got hold of a milking pail and *emboha,* and off they went through the dew-covered grass. Their legs were drenched in dew up to the knees as if they had walked through a river.

Haleera, the elder son, opened for the calves. However, this time the cows did not moo. Most of them lay still and on their stomachs and with their legs stretched out. Others lay down while vomiting incessantly. As for those that stood, from their mouths came stentorian rumbling. Rukundakanuzire stood still, not understanding what was going on. As he was about to move again, his favourite cow, Gaaju, fell and would have hit him had he not been quick to dodge it. The sheep were all gone, as well as some heifers.

Rukundakanuzire and his sons stood transfixed in the middle of the kraal, utterly dumbfounded. No one knew what had happened. The cows kept on falling, some landing on others, as they watched. Still awestruck and confused about what to do, he sent Haleera for his spear. He knew that this outrage had been committed by his nemeses from Banya village - to be exact, Bwengye's sons. Shortly after Haleera had left the kraal, they heard him scream once. Rukundakanuzire rushed to find out what had happened to his son. A stone from nowhere had hit him on the head and he had fallen down in a heap and passed out. As Rukundakanuzire dashed towards his son, he, too, was hit by a ferociously thrown stone and collapsed in a heap.

Baryabusha had come to finish off Rukundakanuzire and his family to avenge his father's disappearance. He had come in the night and fed all the cows on the poisonous peelings and then he had lurked around like a ghost. His mission was to massacre them when they turned up to milk the cows. When the boys saw what had happened to their father, they fled through the hedge of the kraal and hid in the bush.

"You killed my father and hid his body. You also die with your cows and son, idiot!" Baryabusha yelled between sobs and slunk back into the bushes.

When Rukundakanuzire came to, he had a pounding headache.

****

Rukundakanuzire's wife nursed him until he was fine again. The family then left the village with the few cows that had survived and the children. They settled in another village many miles away from Buregyeya.

Rukundakanuzire vowed to exact revenge against Baryabusha. He had lost innumerable cattle and sheep. He had left Buregyeya with only eighty heads of cattle and settled in Mubaya. He was miserable and looked careworn. He had lost his wealth. Now he was nearly among the poorest yet he was once the richest in Buregyeya and the neighbouring villages. He loved his daughter so much that he could kill any male stranger whom he caught trespassing on his compound. His home and its surroundings were out of bounds to any uninvited man who wasn't a relative or close friend. Rukundakanuzire's expectation was that a man would come and officially ask for Bekunda's hand in marriage in exchange for great wealth like cows, goats and sheep. She was stunning and adorable and the effulgence of her skin and curvy figure complemented her beauty well. She was a queen in Mubaya and the surrounding villages across the hills.

One day, Bekunda went to the coffee plantation to collect fallen dry branches for cooking. Her brothers were looking after cattle away from home and her mother was sick. The horny men of the village, who had been lurking around and praying for the day they would get hold of the luscious but barricaded Bekunda, thought to themselves that the day the gods had planned had arrived when they saw her. They drooled at her as she ascended the valley. They drooled like a dog that has seen a piece of meat swinging like a pendulum. Their eyes reddened. They left their rabbit hunting activity and slunk towards the valley to meet the queen of the village who was busy collecting firewood under the coffee trees as she sang. The men got hold of her from behind, gagged her with a piece of cloth and gang-raped her, one by one. They then left her lying unconscious and helpless on the bed of coffee leaves that littered everywhere under the trees.

They ran away thereafter into the fields, laughing, back to their rabbit hunt. Bekunda got up after she had recovered from the post-rape shock. She staggered like a drunken vagabond. Blood was streaming down the insides of her thighs to her feet. She cried loudly but no one was there to listen except the birds and frogs. Using the *lesu* with which she had tied up her hair, she mopped up the blood. When she was satisfied that she was now reasonably clean, she dug into the litter and hid the *lesu*, covering it with more dry leaves. She cursed the bastards that had gang-raped her. She had never been engaged in any intercourse before; this was her first experience. She had been longing for the experience but had not expected that it would be with a gang of randy men. She wished her father was around to kill the bastards. Sons of bitches!

Bekunda collected the wood that had got scattered during the scuffle and rushed back home. When she reached home, she found that her brothers were already back but not her father. However, the smell of tobacco assured her that he was nearby. She neither told her mother nor brothers about what had transpired. It was her nauseous secret. She was naïve and didn't know what to do after such an incident.

Her behaviour suddenly changed. She became withdrawn, unfriendly and rude to everyone at home. Everyone around seemed to be an idiot and she hated herself. She was no longer the Bekunda whom everyone knew, the loving daughter of Rukundakanuzire. Ingabire noticed the change in her daughter's behaviour before everyone else. Conceivably others noticed, too, and chalked it up to adolescence. There was trouble. Her mother vainly spoke to Bekunda a number of times.

Bekunda was pregnant. Ingabire noticed it and could not believe.

"I am always with my daughter. How did she become pregnant? Who could have impregnated her?" Ingabire asked herself, miserably.

Ingabire needed to be sure. She had seen Bekunda vomit behind the kitchen early in the morning, she had noticed her breasts swell abnormally, and she had seen her innumerable times sit in the hot sun.

"I have to do something now," Ingabire said to herself.

****

Darkness settled and everyone gathered in the compound to eat supper. The boys sat with their father and started eating while Ingabire and Bekunda sat in the kitchen around the fire. They also started eating.

"Bekunda, you have changed lately in behavior. I also notice that you are growing fat around the tummy and the breasts are becoming full with milk," Ingabire remarked in between chewing. "Tell me something. Have you slept with any man?" she added after swallowing the food in her mouth.

Bekunda wished to be swallowed up by the fire that leapt and flickered in the middle of three cooking stones. She wished to crumble into particles and disappear into the hearth. Her mother's questions were like an arrow, like Rukundakanuzire's spear that killed Bwengye. She started sweating profusely in the armpits. Beads of sweat started forming on her temples. She couldn't swallow the food she had been chewing. She was taciturn for several minutes, mulling over how to answer her loving mother. She managed to swallow the lump of food in her mouth. And when she had parted the lips to answer, Ingabire interjected impatiently with another string of questions.

"If you do not tell me, I will tell your father, and you well know the consequences," she said rather impatiently.

Bekunda felt a drip of liquid wet her panties. The suggestion of involving her father made her wet herself in fear. She was sweating in the armpits and the sweat had drenched her blouse. She decided to abandon fear and tell the story to her mother, who had started threatening.

By the time Bekunda had finished narrating her ordeal, they were both crying silently in commiseration.

"Why didn't you tell me that day?" Ingabire asked between the sobs. "I would have done something to prevent the negative consequences," she added. "Those fools would have been hunted and killed." She sounded furious, her voice strained.

Bekunda now couldn't ascertain who was responsible for the pregnancy. She was carrying the product of gang rape. As a custom, a lady who gets pregnant before marriage is killed. She is pushed off the top of a cliff by the oldest brother. She loved her life, she feared death, but she never wanted to abort!

She planned to escape the wrath that would ensue - the wrath of the clan, village and parents! She escaped at night the day she learnt that there were plans for her to be killed the following day. She ran following the village paths, crossed the river that separated the villages, wandered through the night and hid at the home of a relative who kindly welcomed and took care of her until she gave birth. The child was a boy.

****

Rukundakanuzire was very furious when he learnt from his wife that Bekunda had disappeared. The turn of events was too much to stomach. One evening, he returned home and beat up everyone until his wife told him everything. What saddened him most was that he didn't know where to start the search for his daughter. He suspected that Baryabusha had come and kidnapped her or that they had eloped. But no, who are these idiots that gang-raped my lovely daughter? Did they include Baryabusha? No. Many unanswered questions ran through his mind. He vowed to visit the famous *murangi* the following day and seek revenge.

He woke up very gloomy on a Saturday morning and told his sons to drive the cattle to the pastures. He didn't care about anything now. All he cared about was the chance to kill the bastards that had gang-raped his daughter. He vowed not to return home until he had found his daughter and had killed her tormentors.

"Bye, daddy," Umwiza said as he departed and waved, but her father was too distracted by anger to pay attention. He had even refused to eat supper. Off he went with his spear in the right hand. He walked for many kilometres until he reached the *murangi*'s home in Rwenshohera village.

The *murangi* welcomed Rukundakanuzire. After they had exchanged pleasantries, he led him behind the house and they walked into the banana plantation, where they sat under the big fig tree.

"I see you have a lot of problems. You are lumbering with huge problems, young man," the decrepit *murangi* remarked, his tone heavy with concern. He reached for his calabash and shook it noisily while uttering incantations. He asked Rukundakanuzire to close his eyes. He rose up and shook the calabash vigorously while strutting around him. He stopped and sat facing Rukundakanuzire. Spit had formed in the corners of his mouth while his skin shone with sweat.

"You killed a man a few years ago who had come to ask for your daughter's hand on behalf of his son. You killed him with that spear. Your daughter was too young then to get married. The man's son revenged by killing your cattle and son. You migrated from the village and settled, miserable, in another village. A few months ago your lovely daughter was gang-raped and she has since disappeared. But I see her heavily pregnant in one of five villages. You want to know the rapists and retaliate and you want your daughter back."

The *murangi* made himself comfortable on the ground and asked Rukundakanuzire to confirm whether his revelations were accurate or not. "The spirits of your forefathers even influence you to wake up in the night and roam around naked. You even eat corpses," he added before Rukundakanuzire could open his mouth to confirm.

Rukundakanuzire was utterly shocked at the man's revelations. His gods were very powerful, he thought to himself. He started trembling and stammered when he attempted to talk.

"Allll yyy- oo-uuu hhhaa hhhaaave sss ssaid iiis true," Rukundakanuzire stuttered. He assured the *murangi* that he was ready to give him anything he wanted if he could help alleviate the plight he was caught up in.

The *murangi* stood up again with calabashes in both hands. This time, he shook the calabashes more vigorously than before. He shuffled around the big tree five times while loudly chanting incantations. When he stopped, he stood still and silence ensued. He carelessly dropped the calabashes on the ground and stood still. Rukundakanuzire was watching with surprise, wondering why the man was delaying the process. While he was still wondering what the next action would be, he saw the *murangi* disappear into the tree. A chill of fright ran down his spine. He jumped up hurriedly and stood still. He considered running away because he had never before seen a human being disappear into a tree. However, he just stood there, looking hither and whither, then again at the tree, with eyes almost popping out of the sockets. As he cast his eyes at the calabashes, they disappeared into the ground. He stood there half-dead, like a robot waiting for a command by remote control. From nowhere, a wind started blowing strongly. It carried off the mulch that covered the ground, sparing only the environs of the sacred place under the fig tree.

Shortly, the wind stopped and the *murangi* suddenly reappeared. He was holding a calabash in each hand and a cow horn nestled under his right armpit. He laughed hysterically at his patient and ordered him to sit down.

"I am from talking to the gods about your situation. The gods need twenty-one sheep and twelve cows. Your problems will be solved," the *murangi* announced. "Go and bring the things I have mentioned tomorrow evening. And don't forget Bekunda's bloodstained clothes that are in the coffee plantation." His voice was strong.

Rukundakanuzire looked on, surprised, and asked, "Where am I going to get the bloodstained cloth?"

"Here," the *murangi* advised, "take this with you. When you reach home, stand in the compound and, with all your energy, throw it into the coffee plantation. Then in the morning go and look for it. If you find it, dig where it will be lying and you will find the clothes there. And make sure no one sees you." The *murangi* handed Rukundakanuzire the cow horn.

Rukundakanuzire set off back home on an empty stomach. The hot laid itself out on him all through the journey. But he was committed to doing anything that would ensure that his problems went away. He reached home at night when everyone was already asleep. He did all the *murangi* had told him to do. When he had finished, he checked on the cows and established that they were okay. He went into the house and slept.

The following day he woke up before anyone else and milked the cows alone. He separated the sheep and the cows that he would take to the *murangi* from those that were to remain. The ones that were to remain he drove out of the kraal and the ones he would take remained behind. He called his sons and when they came, he told them to go and look after the cattle and sheep that he had driven out. They obeyed and ran after the cattle while the sheep ambled behind them. He went to the forest and searched for the horn in vain. He cursed under his breath and thought that the *murangi* wanted to fleece him of his cows and sheep. He gave up the search when the sun had become too hot.

Furious, he vowed not to go back to the *murangi*. He started hitting coffee trees with his spear as he walked back home. One of the trees shook vigorously. A snake fell from the tree on him. He pushed it away with his bare hands and in the process he fell down on a blanket of coffee leaves. Something pricked him. When he examined it, he discovered that it was the same horn the *murangi* had given him. He smiled. Rapidly, he scratched away the litter until he saw the clothes where Bekunda had hidden them that fateful day of the rape. He vigorously shook soil off the clothes and pocketed them. He briskly walked home. He arrived back home panting and breakfasted on the potatoes and yams that Ingabire had prepared and washed them down with a jug of milk. He was satisfied now after two days without eating or drinking anything. He had grown small and old; he had not bathed for days and was stinking like a Matabele ant.

By dusk, Rukundakanuzire was already in the *murangi*'s compound with the cattle, sheep and bloodstained clothes he had been sent for. The *murangi* welcomed him and inspected the sheep and cattle. He picked out one bull and one ewe and instructed his son to drive the others to the kraal. He asked for a knife and his granddaughter brought it to him and he pocketed it. They disappeared into the banana plantation and again went under the big fig tree. The *murangi* sat down and reached for his calabashes, spat into each and closed them both. He instructed Rukundakanuzire to remove his *rugabire*, sit down and close his eyes. He did so with indescribable rapidity. The *murangi* stood and shook the calabashes vigorously with incantations. He started sweating profusely. At the end of the session, his body was all drenched in sweat. He dropped the calabashes on the mulch and disappeared into the tree. After several minutes the bull started sinking into the earth, the calabashes rose on their own and hung up in the branches. Rukundakanuzire started trembling when he stealthily opened his eyes and saw the bull sinking slowly into the hard earth. The ewe started bleating and the *murangi* showed up suddenly. He cut the slit of the ewe and spilt blood on the sinking bull, on the bloodstained cloth and some on Rukundakanuzire. The *murangi* raised his hands and automatically the calabashes fell into both hands. He uttered incantations and handed the calabashes over to Rukundakanuzire.

"You may ask the gods whatever you want now," the *murangi* instructed Rukundakanuzire, who had been trembling with fear.

"I want the spirits of my forefathers to leave me. I want the bastards that raped my daughter to come crawling like snakes to my home. And, finally, I want my daughter to come back home," Rukundakanuzire said, tears running down his cheeks.

He handed over the calabashes back to the *murangi*. The *murangi* shook the calabashes while uttering the incantations and disappeared again into the tree. The earth had swallowed the bull and there was no sign that something as big as a bull had sunk into the soil save for the blood that splattered the mulch. The *murangi* appeared again, this time without his calabashes and donning a fresh set of clothes.

"Your daughter will never come back home, but other things you asked for will happen the day after tomorrow," the *murangi* said. "The gods have told me that your daughter is safer where she is than she would be back in the village where she would die," he added sternly.

"Now get up and walk back to your village. When you reach the river that separates this village from yours, bathe and leave your clothes to float away with the water. Smear yourself with this medicine and sneak back home naked." The *murangi* handed over the powder to Rukundakanuzire. Rukundakazunire nodded in acquiescence and left the *murangi*'s village happy and healed.

****

The village was struck with amazement when, one morning, four men reported in Rukundakanuzire's compound crawling on their tummies and crying for forgiveness. Everyone gathered in his compound to feed their eyes and ears. The whole village thronged into the compound. No one had ever seen such a thing before! The four men were brothers and known hunters in the nearby village of Bulanda. Rukundakanuzire had not reached home. Where was he? No one knew. The four men cried for forgiveness. They had crawled from Bulanda and their tummies, knees, ankles and feet dripped with blood. Ingabire vainly searched for her husband. The day was sunny and the villagers kept thronging into the compound. Those who had come in the morning braved the hot sun up to evening, waiting to see what would happen to the men.

The night Rukundakanuzire left the *murangi*'s village, he reached the river and took off his clothes carefully as he had been told. He bathed. Unfortunately, he threw the clothes into the water before removing the powder from the trouser pocket where he had deposited it. The clothes were carried away by the water. The moon had been full and it shone with pride. He had sat on a stone and started scooping water with both hands and bathing himself while singing. Suddenly, he realised that he had forgotten to remove the powder from his trouser pocket. He had seen the clothes floating slowly away. He had dived into the water to try and catch the clothes. Not knowing how to swim, he had gone down. In the twilight between life and death, he had seen the spirits of his forefathers on the bank of the river. They had upbraided and cursed him for desecrating the agreement they had made with his father. He had pleaded with them in vain, and they had laughed at him without compunction.

Rukundakanuzire had given up on the possibility that he might still live. While the tide of water pushed him about helplessly, he had hit his head on a stone that jutted out in the water. He had turned and hit his back on another stone. He had bounced like a ball and fallen on yet another with his tummy. He had thrown up all the water he had swallowed.

At last, he was able to breathe again. He opened his eyes. The spirits had been laughing endlessly on the bank of the river, throwing all sorts of insults at him. He could hardly stand up. He managed to turn his head and saw his clothes stuck on a stone near him. He managed to stretch his arm and pull them to where he lay. When he had checked in the trouser and found the powder still intact in the polythene bag, he opened it and smeared himself. The spirits disappeared instantly. He threw the clothes back into the water and passed out!

He was woken up by arrows of the morning sun. He had gathered himself up and climbed the bank of the river and rested under a tree. Hunger prodded him to get up. He was staggering but managed to journey on under the full moon. He reached his village when night was separating with day. He was naked. He decided to hide in the coffee plantation until the night. That was when he would sneak into the house when no one was looking.

He was not surprised when he reached his compound and found the men lying prostrate there. They had been there since the previous day. The home was silent like a cemetery. He walked slowly and entered the house, rummaged through the bag and got himself a pair of trousers and a shirt. He picked up his spear and sauntered out again. Ingabire followed him. He reached where the four men were lying and pricked them on the buttocks with his spear. They had cried and shed tears until the sockets had run out of liquid. They lay there like corpses. The following morning, he called the chief of the village to decide on what to do to the rapists. They were all carried away and dumped into the river.

Bekunda was very beautiful but lazy. She never wanted to engage in house chores and would often shirk going to the garden with others. She would pretend to be sick every morning but in the afternoons she would be well enough to clean out her plate of food. She was good at malingering, and this spoilt her relationship with the people who had welcomed her when she ran away from her father's home. She was a dirty woman, too, who never minded about her hygiene. She would wake up in the morning, face the mirror and remove rheum from the eyes using a handkerchief instead of washing the whole face, comb the hair and breastfeed her son, Kayibanda. To examine whether she needed to bathe or not, Bekunda would raise her hands and tilt his head towards both armpits and smell them. Only when they smelt foul would she bathe. Frequently, she would wash only the armpits, the undersides of her succulent boobs, her buttocks and the area between the legs. She barely brushed her teeth and, as for the fingernails, she often simply bit them off to make them short.

When the news that the men who had raped her had been apprehended and killed reached her ears, she vowed never to return to her father's village. She regretted why she had protested when her mother had suggested an abortion. "Now my child is fatherless," she thought to herself and tears formed in her eyes. She closed the eyes and drops of tears fell into her open cleavage. Kayibanda looked like his grandfather, Rukundakanuzire, the only difference being that his lips fully covered his teeth. One day, Bekunda thought of going to the market to buy clothes for both herself and for the boy. Kayibanda was now four years old. She would send him to bring or do anything any time. The market was three villages away. It was a Saturday morning when Bekunda got up and started the journey to the market, with Kayibanda perched on her back, tied with a baby shawl stopping at the neck and with his legs embracing

Bekunda's waist almost to the belly button. She clutched him with her hands. They walked without resting through the valleys and hills. They eventually reached the market when the sun was very hot. All through the journey, Kayibanda had been sleeping.

Bekunda untied the knot of the shawl and slid Kayibanda down. Her back where Kayibanda's mouth had been resting was wet with his saliva. The wet patch was big but Bekunda didn't notice it since she couldn't see her back. She settled with her son down in the shade under a big tree and enjoyed the cool and chilly breeze. The market had just opened and a few people were already displaying clothes. More were selling food, especially *katogo* cooked in large saucepans under the burning sun. She yawned when the smell of generously spiced food hit her nostrils. She sprang up to her feet and, with Kayibanda's hand locked in hers, they walked to where the *katogo* was being sold. They greeted the people around the cooking area and sat on a vacated bench near the woman selling the *katogo*. She was busy scooping food from the saucepan onto the plates for the noisy customers.

"How much is a plate of food?" Bekunda asked loudly, looking into the big saucepan.

"One shilling," the woman answered, while scooping some food from the saucepan and dropping it in a heap on a plate.

She patted it gently with another smaller plate and gave the plate with the mound of food to a waiting customer. She received the money from him and stowed it away in the pocket patched onto the dirty apron that was splattered with *matooke* sap and bean soup.

"Give us two plates, one full and the other half for the child," Bekunda ordered.

She casually watched as the old woman bent over the saucepan, with the head disappearing inside it and the left hand clutching the thin rim of the saucepan.

The old woman scooped out the food with one plate and nonchalantly dropped it on a bigger plate. She dipped the hand again in the saucepan and scooped and half-filled a small plate. She again scooped and added broth to both plates.

"Here, get the food and pay," she said while handing Bekunda two plates of food. Bekunda received the plates and put them down on the grass. She dipped her hand into her bra, removed some money and paid. By the time they finished eating, the market was fully packed with people. She got up and held Kayibanda by one hand, helping him to stand up. They sauntered towards the clothing section. When she arrived there she started rummaging through the heap of clothes, searching for what suited Kayibanda. She bought him two oversized T-shirts and two corduroy shorts.

"These ones he will be growing into before I get money to buy others. I cannot buy those that fit him snugly. After three months he will be needing others yet I earn little from selling crops," Bekunda said, the folded clothes already placed in the bag slung over her shoulder.

"Yeah, you are right about being frugal. As for me, I buy clothes for my children only once a year, when I have harvested and sold coffee beans," a plump woman who was also rummaging through a heap agreed with Bekunda.

She darted about the open-air market, looking for where adult clothing was sold, so that she could also buy herself some dresses. Her eyes landed on Ingabire, who was passing at the opposite end of the market, holding a basket. She had last seen her mother several years before when she had escaped from the village, when she was still pregnant with Kayibanda. She quickly picked up her son and threw him on her back like a monkey escaping from an attack. She then picked up the bag containing the clothes she had bought for Kayibanda, which she had put on the ground, and ran towards where Ingabire had passed. She forced her way through a sea of people without minding where she stepped. Her eyes were fixed on her mother who was already about to disappear in a crowd of people.

Ingabire could not believe it when she turned to see who had tapped her back.

She shed tears of joy and gathered both Bekunda and Kayibanda up into her arms.

"Oh my Bekunda, I have been planning to visit you at the aunt's place. What are you doing here? Oh my dear, I missed you! My goodness, I have seen you finally!' Ingabire exclaimed as some saliva escaped from her mouth and hit Bekunda in the face. "Follow me. Let's go," she instructed as she led the way towards a nearby shop.

Ingabire looked back and grabbed Kayibanda away from Bekunda. "Wow, this is undoubtedly Rukundakanuzire," she joyously yelled as they walked on.

She led Bekunda and her son into a house where she owned a shop selling cow ghee and *amacunda*. She used the back room as a bedroom where she lived with Umwiza.

"Here, sit down," she cooed as she pointed to the bench and disappeared into the bedroom.

Bekunda couldn't believe that she had finally connected with her mother after such a long time of not seeing each other. When Ingabire came back from the bedroom, she carried two mugs full of amacunda. She handed one mug to Kayibanda and the other to Bekunda.

"Where is Daddy?" Bekunda asked with impatience.

"Oh my girl, we will have enough time together now that we have found each other. Finish taking that first and we shall talk some more later," she answered, rather exasperated.

"Did something bad happen, Mum?" Bekunda retorted.

"Nothing bad really happened but I broke with your father," she murmured. Bekunda noticed that her mother was shedding tears.

"I am sorry, Mama. Stop crying, Mama, please stop crying," Bekunda urged. Rukundakanuzire had started drinking heavily. Every morning, he would walk to the bar and drink himself silly. Sometimes he would drink until he passed out. The villagers would then call Ingabire, who would go with her sons and carry him back home. The cows had reduced in number. He would defecate in his trousers and she had gotten tired and felt humiliated about having to carry a mature person every day from the bar.

The goings-on in Rukundakanuzire's family had become the subject of discussion in the whole village. Some thought that he was running insane. Some others thought that the ghosts of the four men who had crawled into his compound and reported themselves for raping Bekunda had come back to haunt him. Many theories were used to describe his situation by many people. He had become a villain and laughing stock.

One day, Ingabire decided she couldn't tolerate this nonsense anymore and shut Rukundakanuzire up inside the house. That day he wanted to sell off five cows. He kicked the door open and descended on Ingabire with kicks and punches in the face. In the scuffle, Ingabire lost three teeth and broke an arm. He sprained her spine when he pushed her against the wall, leaving her lying restless and helpless.

Ingabire had since run away from home with Umwiza to Mweera town in the north where her sister lived. Ingabire had met a group of missionaries who proselytised her into adopting Christianity. She had worked as a labourer in a rich man's rice garden where she saved enough money to start up the business of making ghee and *amacunda*.

Bekunda vowed not to go back to her aunt's place. She wished to stay with her mother and search for a man to marry her. She claimed that she had been suffering in her aunt's hands, that she had been subjected to non-stop labour in the banana plantation yet she wasn't given enough to eat. She lied to cajole Ingabire into accepting to stay with her and not send her back. Ingabire loved her daughter very much. She would accept everything she told her, whether truth or lies. They lived together in a two-roomed house. At night, Bekunda and her son would lay down their bedding in the shop and in the morning the bedding would be removed and taken into Ingabire's bedroom. Ingabire was earning enough from the sales of *amacunda* and ghee to take care of them.

Bekunda resorted to prostitution to earn a living. Undoubtedly, she was a head-turner. She therefore looked down on several men because none had the qualities she wanted in a man for marriage. She fell in love several times with different men, who just used and dumped her. The ones she often liked showed little inclination to marry her, yet the ones she did not love often proposed marriage. She was confused. She did not know what to do. She therefore decided to welcome men basing on their worth; you would not bed her for free. She started offering sex in exchange for money. Many men with cash to spare looked for her because she was beautiful and attractive. She did this without her mother knowing and she vowed that no one would stop her. Her thirst for money was unquenchable and she soon saved enough to be able to leave Ingabire's house.

One morning, when Ingabire had gone to buy milk, Bekunda packed her belongings and disappeared with her child. She had stayed with Ingabire for only eight months. She disappeared to another town in the north where she settled as a professional prostitute.

Bekunda loved her son Kayibanda so much that she would not leave him behind. He was her treasure. She got a single-roomed house - or *muzigo* - where she settled with her son. During the day she would sleep and in the evening clean herself and then put on skimpy dresses that clearly displayed her smooth thighs and gorgeous legs. She would stand at the roadside and many men would lay her in exchange for money. In a single night she would serve around thirty men, charging each one five shillings. One day Bekunda left her son sleeping in the house alone and went to do business at the roadside as usual. Immediately she reached the roadside, she found other ladies who were engaged in the same trade as her. She was approached by a short, plump, bearded man, who led her behind a trailer truck and bargained with her for the price for the whole night.

"One hundred and fifty, sir," she said.

"I have one hundred shillings, please, beautiful woman," the man offered.

"If you cannot afford my price, then no business," Bekunda retorted, walking away.

He held her hand and agreed to pay her the amount, besides buying her supper. They walked together and disappeared into a nearby lodge.

Her colleagues in the trade were not happy. Bekunda had arrived late when they were already there. Still it was her, not them, who had got a customer already – within a mere two minutes of waiting. They plotted against Bekunda. She was new on the street but she would serve between fifteen and thirty customers a single night yet they hardly served between two and seven customers a night even though they charged less than she did.

****

The day Bekunda departed, Ingabire arrived back home only to find the house closed. She had left Bekunda cooking some food on the stove on the veranda but now the food was burning. She quickly added some water to the burning food and rushed inside the house. Her daughter's belongings were not there! Only Umwiza was inside, sleeping peacefully.

"Where has she gone now? And why with all her clothes and her son? And why didn't she inform me?" she wondered. "Ehhh, but I have not mistreated her! Has she gone to her aunt or back to her father? Oh, my daughter!"

Her eyes flooded with tears that flowed down her cheeks and fell onto her chest and some onto her feet. She wailed loudly and her neighbours showed up to see what was happening. They sympathised with her and urged her not to worry. Perhaps Bekunda had eloped with a man since she had been seen several times with different men.

****

Kayibanda was six years old now. He would spend his days playing with other children in the neighbourhood while his mother would be sleeping. He only returned home when he was hungry and wanted to sleep. He would leave home in the morning and come back for lunch, go back to play some more and return at night to eat supper and sleep. This was the routine, and it never changed. He enjoyed such unencumbered freedom because his mother had no time to limit his movements. She would come back at dawn and sleep up to lunch time. Then she would get up to cook something to eat and then return to bed. She would sleep again up to six. After that she would prepare supper quickly, clean herself and go on the streets. She would make sure that her son was already asleep before leaving the house. Then she would lock him inside before she left.

Kayibanda was a morbid bed-wetter. Every day Bekunda would come back to be greeted by streams of urine at the doorway. And when she opened the door, the stench would rise through the door into her nostrils. Every day Kayibanda would receive strokes of the cane as a punishment for wetting the mat. The colour of the papyrus mat had changed to coffee brown from lime green owing to the constant assault by urine.

The other girls had been out of business ever since Bekunda had joined them on the streets. Every man around was yearning to spend a night with her. The competition was unbearable. They finally hatched a plan to either disfigure Bekunda so that she was no longer attractive or exterminate her. They contributed some money and bought everything they needed to carry out the mission. They then met the next evening to agree on the best venue to carry out the mission.

The day they should have put their plan in motion, it poured with rain, and at first they thought that their evil plan had been foiled. Soon they realised that the rain was an opportunity to execute their plan and get away without a trace.

They decided to brave the rain and track down Bekunda in the slum where she resided. One of the girls knew the slum quite well so she led them to the *muzigo* where she lived. They were equipped with a small jerrican of acid and some had clubs, *emihini,* in their hands.

Since Bekunda's arrival, they had become like off-layers: they could no longer afford to buy themselves nice clothes or food. They desperately needed to sell again, but that could only happen once the only barrier had been eliminated. They found Bekunda's *muzigo* locked from the outside with a big Solex padlock. They stood on the veranda disappointed and exasperated, they looked as if they were cultivating the next course of action. They stared into the dark rain-spattered night, not knowing what to do next.

Bekunda suddenly showed up running in the heavy rain. Her head was covered with a jacket, which was quite big and covered even the upper part of her body. She had been made visible by the lightning that illuminated the dark night.

When the women saw her, they heaved a collective sigh of relief. They knew that they would now be able to execute their mission without anyone intervening since it was raining and everyone else had taken refuge in their houses. Uwiimana, who had led the group to Bekunda's home, was the first to hit Bekunda on the head with *omuhini* as soon as she set foot on the veranda. She had been hit as soon as she uncovered her head and shook the water off the jacket. Bekunda fell down in a thud like a sack of Irish potatoes. Other girls followed, hitting Bekunda without caring which part they struck, as if she was a snake! She let out a deafening shriek that woke up the neighbours. One of the attackers was struggling to open the jerrican that contained the acid when she heard a clanking on the next door. A neighbour was opening the door in response to the scream. In panic, she dropped the jerrican and took off, followed by her peers, and disappeared into the darkness.

Bekunda had fallen down from the veranda and lay helplessly in the puddles of water. She was wailing with excruciating pain. Bizimungu, who was still shocked at what he saw, still stood at the threshold of his dwelling, his eyes wide open, watching the direction that the gang of ladies had taken. He quickly tightened the towel around the waist and pulled Bekunda up out of the water. He made her sit on the veranda and reached for the key he had seen near her bag to open the door. No sooner had he taken his hands off the bedraggled Bekunda than she lost control and fell again and rolled back into the puddles like a log. He quickly opened the door and rushed out again to try and save the lady. In the process the towel loosened and fell off. He quickly picked it up and wrapped it tightly around his waist. He lifted Bekunda with difficulty. When he had entered the *muzigo* he stumbled and fell and she fell on top of him.

Kayibanda had been dead asleep. He was only awakened by his wailing mother. Bizimungu gathered himself up and helped Bekunda onto the bed. Kayibanda looked stoical. He didn't know why his mother was crying. He only saw, through sleepy eyes, a man who was carrying his mother falling down in a heap, and that they were both bedraggled and drenched with water. He didn't understand what was going on.

When it had stopped raining heavily, Bizimungu mobilised other people and carried Bekunda on a stretcher to the hospital, which was a few kilometres away from the slum. Bekunda had lost eight front teeth, she had broken ribs and one arm was amputated.

During the scuffle one girl had hit her on the joint between the arm and the shoulder, dislocating it. Her left ear was also shattered and blood oozed through it, and this scared the doctors, who thought she would not survive. She spent about five months in a coma at the missionary hospital.

Bizimungu had taken over the responsibility to look after Kayibanda and would frequently come with him to the hospital during all the months Bekunda was there. He would cry heavily, thinking his mother was going to die. When Bekunda regained consciousness, the first word she uttered was her son's name.

"Kayib-bba-nn-da...," she stammered painfully as she opened her eyes.

No one was around in the room. She wondered where she was and what she was doing there. She tried to sit up. However, the pain was still too much. She cried out and collapsed back onto the bed.

The Bekunda who eventually got out of the hospital was a caricature of the Bekunda who had escaped from her mother and come to engage in prostitution in this town. She now had only one ear, one arm, she was thin and her hair had been cut off. When she looked at herself in the mirror, she wished she had instead been killed. She looked like an old chicken that had been dipped in water. With such disfigured looks, she believed that her career in prostitution was no more. The gang of girls she called her friends had won the battle against her. She hated the country now.

She planned to pack up with her son and escape to a neighbouring country. The thought of going back to her father or mother was scary. She needed to go somewhere very far where no one knew her. The border with the country to which she wanted to run was near. It was only one day's walk through the forests and many refugee camps. She never planned to pass through the official border posts because the army would force her into a refugee camp. She would be refused permission to get out of the country. So she hatched a plan to use the *panya* routes in Buyoyo Forest and cross Mahurunguru River and then proceed to Kalenga country.

She shed rivers of tears whenever she remembered the gang of men on top of her, forcing their way into her in the coffee plantation. She regretted why she had kept what had happened to her a secret when the consequences were guaranteed to be so harsh and force her out of the village so that she would have to seek refuge in another village. She wailed uncontrollably, her heart full of regret about her escape from her caring and loving mother. Had she settled down and accepted one of the men who had begged to marry her, she would be happily married now. But materialism had made her blind; her beauty had made her feel that she owned the world.

How wrong she had been! She had hammered the last nail into her coffin when she had chosen prostitution as her career. It was prostitution that had blinded her into abandoning her caring mother and into escaping with Kayibanda to the town in the farthest north. It was because of prostitution that other ladies had felt so jealous of her that they had wanted to finish her off. And it was prostitution that had made her lose an ear, an arm and some of her teeth. When she smiled, you would think it's the aerial view of a clearing in the middle of a forest. She now lisped. She now pronounced 'abaserikale' as 'abatherikale' and 'sitaane' as 'thitaane'. There was now no way she could cajole any man to sleep with her - not even in exchange for a coin! Her beautiful figure eight had shrunk the four months she had been laid up in the hospital. Now when she walked, one would mistake her for a scarecrow in a cornfield. Bekunda nearly lost her mind as she immersed in thoughts of her past life. She thought about committing suicide. However, thoughts about her lovely son, Kayibanda, soothed her emotions somewhat.

After Bekunda had healed well, she got up in the middle of the night, when everyone was sleeping. She decided to escape to another country where no one knew her. She got out of her house, leaving the door open to avoid suspicion from neighbours. She knew they would get suspicious upon hearing the door slamming. She began the trek with her son perched on her back as she held him with her only arm. Kayibanda was the only possession Bekunda had now, and she vowed to protect him with all her might and watch him grow into a man. She walked under the full moon. She didn't carry anything from the house.

"Mama, where are we going now?" Kayibanda asked curiously.

"We are going to see Kuuku and Shwenkuru," she responded. Then she coughed and spat lumps of phlegm into the bush.

"Why don't we wait and go there in the morning, Mama? The lion will eat us," Kayibanda murmured fearfully.

Bekunda was lost for words. She could not immediately answer Kayibanda's inquisitive questions and decided to keep quiet for a few minutes as she meditated on what answers to give. Kayibanda had started snoring on her back.

She was relieved when she heard the susurration of snores emanating from her son. She journeyed on and on through the village paths until she reached the edge of the forest and rested under the big tree. Kayibanda was already in dreamland when he was put down and covered with a *lesu*. Bekunda sat beside Kayibanda, who lay asleep. Her buttocks were level with her feet and her chin rested on her knees. Her only hand wildly scratched the itching spot on the leg where a hungry mosquito had pierced and sucked blood stealthily. With her breath, she shooed away the many buzzing mosquitoes that were hovering over her. Shortly after, she fell asleep and started snoring.

Bekunda's sleep was cut short by the ebullient birds and their boisterous chirping. Some of the birds were perched on different tree branches. Cranes in four pairs were wandering about the nearby swamp, picking up the jumping insects. The marabou storks made the loudest noise, perched in the tree beside the one they slept under. They chirped noisily and shat stinking white dung that turned the whole grass under the tree white. It was dawn. When Bekunda raised her head and opened her sleepy eyes, she saw beads of dew on blades of grass. The sun had risen from behind the mountains and it threw weak arrows of rays on her and her son. The rays were ineffectual. She wished for stronger rays because she had spent the night without covering herself and she was feeling very cold. She yawned and cast her eyes where Kayibanda had been sleeping. He was still enjoying his sleep. However, the *lesu* she had covered him with had fallen off and was now in the grass near him. The area where they lay under the tree had no dew. She moved, crouching, to where Kayibanda lay and woke him up. She helped him stand and examined the rash on his left cheek. Mosquitoes had pierced him with their sharp proboscises and ravenously sucked blood from him, and thus the rash. She squatted and put him on her back. She then got back up on her feet, ready to trudge on through the forest and to the river. Kayibanda yawned and demanded *chai* and food. He was hungry and wanted something to eat. He wasn't in the least aware of the quagmire they were entangled in. He thought it was the usual situation of waking up early morning to eat leftovers before washing his face.

"We shall find guavas and oranges up ahead, my dear. Be strong like a man," Bekunda comforted him.

"Okay, Mama," Kayibanda said as he yawned.

Bekunda was also hungry. Her prayer was that she would come across a guava tree or wild berries in the forest in which they were wandering. She walked and walked until she got tired. She put Kayibanda down and they walked together hand in hand. They found a garden of cassava and she uprooted one plant. It had three tubers. She broke them off from the stem and then sat down with her son. They ate the cassava until they were satisfied and re-energised for the journey.

Without any mishaps, they reached the bank of Mahurunguru River, which separates Kalenga from Muhemba. They could not figure out how to cross because there was no bridge and they didn't know how to swim. She ambled on the banks, hoping to find stones over which they could walk and cross the river. Kayibanda trotted behind Bekunda with difficulty. He was haggard. He was not aware of the conundrum that they were caught up in. His mother had assured him that they were going to see Kuuku and Shwenkuru but they seemed to be taking forever reaching them. With impatience registering on his face, he thought that perhaps they had lost their way. Finally, Bekunda found the shallow area with stones jutting out where they could easily walk across the river to Kalenga. She thought that the country she was leaving was not meant to be hers, considering the many mazes and the deep suffering she had gone through. When she had crossed the river into Kalenga, she sighed in relief and vowed never to return to her cursed country. She thought about her father and mother with sadness, then about her siblings. She wished they had come with her.

Bekunda and Kayibanda now needed shelter where they could rest for a while and decide what to do next. They needed food and clothes. Their stomachs were empty and their tattered clothes had been torn by the thorn trees and grass that they had brushed through on their journey. She had nowhere to start from. Her capacity to think coherently was exhausted. She had crossed the Rubicon now that she had set foot in the country she desired. She believed that she had run away from problems and had now entered a realm of happiness. She had not known that she was jumping from the pan directly into the fire. She knelt down for Kayibanda to climb onto her back. Then she got up and walked through the bush and started climbing a hill. When she reached the top of the hill, she saw another hill dotted with settlements and separated by a verdant valley of swamps and shrubs. They were hungry and Kayibanda had started crying again. They were careworn and could not manage to walk any further. She collapsed and slept. Kayibanda no longer had any tears to shed when he saw his mother collapse in a heap. He followed suit and slept near her. In no time, they were both snoring. The condition they were in now, they were inclined to accept every situation - like a latrine that accepts all kinds of dung, whether big or small.

Part Two

A nomadic pastoralist had been driving his cattle from where he had watered them under the scorching sun back to the fields for the cows to graze some more. That was when he noticed the two figures - a woman and child - lying still like stones. He stopped whistling and stood still, wondering what such vulnerable people were looking for in the wilderness far away from the nearest settlements. He got frightened and many questions ran through his head. He put down a jerrican that had *macunda*, the dish and the *enkoni*. He picked up a stone of reasonable size that he knew he would manage to throw where the two figures lay. He drew back his arm and threw the stone at another big one near where they lay. The impact produced a clanking, deafening noise. Kayibanda got up, frightened, and attempted to run, but fell down immediately. He looked very sleepy and bits of straw stuck to his cheeks.

"Do not beat us, please sir," Kayibanda screamed, scared.

He looked unblinking at the man. He added apologetically, "We are going to visit Kuuku and Shwenkuru but we are tired, hungry and lost."

The pastoralist got close. Indeed the young man's lips were parched and they had cracked from hunger and the scorching sun. Bekunda had been listening and watching but didn't have the energy to gather herself up or utter a word. The pastoralist walked back, bringing milk and potato leftovers, and he gave them generous amounts. He sat on a big stone and sympathetically watched from a distance as, still lying, Bekunda and Kayibanda ate and drank voraciously as if they had never seen food and milk before. They soon finished.

"Come on, follow me and I will help you," the pastoralist said as he got up to go. The pastoralist's name was Kagurutsi. He wandered everywhere looking for pasture and would leave one area during drought to settle in another place where the pasture was greener. He had no permanent settlement. Whenever he would reach a place that he liked, he would cut poles and build a hut and thatch it with grass, a kraal for his cows and a small shed for the calves. He had lost his father and mother to dysentery in the same year that he had lost his wife. When he was widowed, they had a five-year-old child, who also soon disappeared from him. He had left Biguri village where he had lived with his wife for twenty years and wandered around until he found beautiful Malanga village. The village had enough water for the animals and for human use. River Mahurunguru flowed gurgling day in, day out, year in, year out, without drying.

Kagurutsi led satisfied Kayibanda and Bekunda to his hut and instructed them to feel free and rest and then continue with their journey when they felt energised and fresh. Bekunda felt relieved and slept off. Kayibanda was excited about the new environment and the cows. He failed to rest and went to the calves that were kept in a shed and excitedly stared at them. He followed Kagurutsi to the fields and helped him graze the cows. Kayibanda loved animals and he was voluble. Kagurutsi enjoyed his company that evening and it cured his loneliness.

When Kagurutsi and Kayibanda came back home that evening, Bekunda was sitting on an anthill, visibly lost in thought. She had slept and refreshed herself and was now wondering where to go. She had no destination in mind. She was like a butterfly that flutters in any direction in which the wind takes it, like water that flows day and night looking for level ground to settle. Kagurutsi made a fire and they all sat around it and started roasting matooke and cassava. They ate in silence and drank milk. Kayibanda was already dozing with food in his hands and mouth until Bekunda lifted him up to the hut. She came back and sat with Kagurutsi around the fire and continued to eat in silence.

"What happened to your arm, ear and teeth?" Kagurutsi suddenly asked Bekunda as he poked the embers with a piece of wood and sparks flew up, crackling, to form a fountain.

"I fell off a mango tree and broke the arm, and it was amputated," Bekunda lied, her voice low. Immediately her face dropped. She looked at the fire and faked a cough.

"What about the ear and the teeth?" Kagurutsi inquired, in a strained voice, giving her a serious look.

"My father came back home drunk and started beating my mother. When I went to separate them he hit me on the mouth with his fist and the teeth fell out," Bekunda said. "He then followed me where I had fallen and chopped off my ear as a warning never to interfere in a parents' fight," she added while rubbing her eyes with the back of her hand as she faked sobs.

They talked for a long time. At the end, Bekunda confessed that they were not headed anywhere specific, that they had run away from their home because her father had threatened to chop them to pieces with a machete just like one would chop cabbage or onions. Kagurutsi believed her without question. He offered to keep Bekunda and her son until she got where to go.

Bekunda wondered at the generosity of this stranger named Kagurutsi. She reproached herself inside her heart for lying about what happened to her but vowed to never reveal her secret. She now had a home to stay and food to eat together with her son.

Kagurutsi dropped another log into the fire and the red sparks from the embers shimmered in the darkness. Kagurutsi and Bekunda moved into the hut and slept. The hut consisted of only one room and contained a bed made of straw and papyrus where Kagurutsi slept. Bekunda and her son slept down on the bare floor.

The following day Kagurutsi cut some grass and made for Bekunda and Kayibanda a mattress. He put this mattress down on the floor so that they could sleep comfortably. Kayibanda was a bed wetter, so every morning Bekunda would put out the yellowish grass, drenched in urine, to dry. Almost every week she would replace the grass with newly cut and dried one. Soon the part of the floor where Kayibanda slept sagged and formed a pothole due to his urine's effect.

Bekunda's stay with Kayibanda at Kagurutsi's humble home turned out to be a blessing for both. Kagurutsi fed them like they were his own flesh and blood whilst Kayibanda was very comfortable with Kagurutsi as if he was his father. Kagurutsi taught him how to milk the cows, how to dig the anthill for fresh brown soil and smear it on the *bwaato* every day and pour water into it for the cattle to drink. He would do all that freely and rapidly. Kagurutsi treated Kayibanda like his own son and he loved him.

With time, Kayibanda forgot about where he had been told that they were going and stopped asking. He had become comfortable waking up early in the morning and milking cows with Kagurutsi and driving the cattle out to the fields. He loved the routine and that made him forget about Kuuku and Shwenkuru. Bekunda drank a lot of milk and enjoyed the food. She, too, had started to feel comfortable around Kagurutsi. However, she was confused about what to call him. Bekunda's admirable figure had started to recuperate from shrinking. The killer curves had begun to show again and she was beginning to look normal. She would never get her arm and teeth back, but the rest of the body was slowly regaining its shape and, with time, she would be attractive again.

One day, when Bekunda and her son had now spent two months with Kagurutsi, the man left Kayibanda tending the animals and returned home to rest. He was feeling unwell. He carried different types of leaves and roots with him. When he arrived back home, he requested Bekunda to crush the leaves and roots and squeeze out juice into a cup. He entered the hut and lay on his bed complaining of stomach ache. Bekunda crushed the herbs and roots in the mortar with a pestle and squeezed the juice out of them into the cup with her hand as she had been told. She managed to get a cupful of juice from the crushed leaves and roots. She took the juice to Kagurutsi, who lay on the bed writhing and groaning in pain. She handed to him the cup and he gulped down the contents, including the dregs. Then he handed the cup back to her and she sauntered back out. Kagurutsi noticed something when Bekunda handed him the cup full of medicine. When she bent to hand over the cup, the succulent boobs almost popped out of the blouse Bekunda wore. Kagurutsi watched and felt like touching the beautiful smooth breasts. When she was sauntering out, he saw her thighs through the light skirt she wore and felt his heart jolt like it had been hit by lightning. It had been long since he last slept with a woman. The sight of Bekunda had, however, reignited feelings that he had long forgotten. He thought back to the Bekunda he had found almost dead in the grass, emaciated and ugly, and compared her with the Bekunda who had just brought him medicine. He concluded that these were two entirely different women.

"Ehh, the woman is beautiful though she has some missing body parts!" he whispered to himself, then whistled in exclamation.

He immediately felt healed. He got up and walked out of the hut. He found Bekunda giving the calves water.

"Let us go and look for food," he suggested. "I am feeling better now."

Bekunda nodded in acquiescence and smiled. The smile exposed her toothless black gums and two beautiful dimples on her cheeks.

Kagurutsi, holding a machete, led the way and Bekunda followed. Off they went to the garden to get some potatoes and oranges.

"Bekunda, I want you to stay here with me; I don't want you to go," Kagurutsi offered. "You are beautiful and I love you and your son Kayibanda. Ever since you came to stay with me, I have felt comfortable and secure. I no longer feel bereft," Kagurutsi added and turned to look at Bekunda.

Bekunda was confounded by Kagurutsi's sudden utterance because she had not seen it coming. She had not for any one moment expected that Kagurutsi would fall in love with her.

"Are you thuwa of what you're theying?" Bekunda lisped through her missing teeth. She felt coy.

"Yes, I am serious. Please be my wife," he proposed and proceeded to hold her hand.

"We thall talk about it over za fire tonight," she suggested and pulled her hand away from his grip. Kagurutsi didn't answer. They had already reached the garden.

Because Bekunda had only one arm, she suggested that she picks the oranges as Kagurutsi digs out the potatoes with the machete. Bekunda walked towards the tree and saw many ripe oranges but she hardly reached the branches. She stood on her toes to gain more height in order to reach the oranges. She had, unfortunately, not seen the thorns on the orange tree. The thorns hooked into the dress as she stretched out, but she did not immediately realize it. It's as she attempted to move another tree after picking three fruits from the first one that she realized that her dress had been hooked. In the struggle to remove the thorns violently, the dress was pulled down and it fell to the ground. She cried for help and Kagurutsi rushed to where she was. Kagurutsi couldn't believe what he was seeing! Beside the orange tree stood a woman with one hand and one ear but who had the figure and skin of an angel, and her succulent breasts were like those of a virgin. Kagurutsi's trousers started bulging. Bekunda felt shy and covered her breasts with her arm. Though the dress had come off her body some of it remained hooked on the thorns.

Kagurutsi got closer. However, instead of helping her unhook the dress, he hugged her and kissed her on the lips. His whiskers were sharp and untrimmed and she felt them on her nose. She never protested. He undressed himself quickly and made love to her right there on the grass. When they finished, they joined hands in searching for fruits. As Kagurutsi picked and threw down the fruits, Bekunda picked them up and deposited them in a basket which already contained potatoes. Kagurutsi carried the harvested fruits on his head while Bekunda carried only the machete and they walked back home.

Bekunda became Kagurutsi's wife and Kayibanda became their son. Kayibanda easily got assimilated into the situation because he had never seen his father, so he innocently believed that Kagurutsi was his biological father. He obeyed and loved him as much as he would have loved his own father. The trio were now a happy family. Kayibanda was happy; Bekunda was happy; and so was Kagurutsi. The happiest, however, was Kayibanda because he enjoyed the wilderness life of being with cows and sheep. He enjoyed eating roast meat every time a cow or sheep died. Kagurutsi would slaughter the animal with his machete and give some of the meat to Bairu who helped him till the land and plant food. Bekunda grew more and more beautiful. She became more beautiful than every other woman in the village despite her physical limitations. She wished she had met Kagurutsi when she was still complete. However, she knew that her penchant for opulence and luxury and her greed for money had made her turn down innumerable marriage proposals. She had instead chosen prostitution, the result of which was that she was now disabled. She knew she would live to regret that decision her whole life.

Bekunda started missing her mother, father, and siblings. But she had vowed never to return to the cursed country. Kayibanda was growing at an indescribable pace. Their condition was now okay. Where else do you get such a man in the world who loves you unconditionally? Bekunda thought to herself.

One night, cattle rustlers attacked Malanga village to steal cattle from the pastoralists. Kagurutsi was woken up by the deafening wailing '*wala' lalala!*' noise from the neighbours. He quickly got out of the hut and Kayibanda followed him, carrying his *nkoni*. When Kagurutsi noticed that they were faced with rustlers, he instructed

Kayibanda to return inside the house and hide there. When the rustlers reached the compound, Kagurutsi was standing under a tree. He changed into a huge lion and scared away the rustlers. Kayibanda was watching. He got very scared when he saw his father change into a lion. He thought that one day, he might turn into a lion and eat them while they were asleep. Kagurutsi quickly changed back into a human and whistled in victory. Kayibanda quickly ran back to his bed when he noticed that Kagurutsi had now got close to the house.

Kagurutsi was a direct descendant of the Bachwezi. He would turn into anything he wanted to protect his cattle or himself when attacked. He had done so several times.

A few days later, Kayibanda begged his father to teach him how to change into a lion and Kagurutsi promised to teach him when he grew up. He promised to take him to the headquarters of Bachwezi for embrocation and proselytisation into the belief. Kayibanda agreed. He felt impatient and wished he could grow up very fast such that they could go to the headquarters the following day.

Kayibanda was an ambitious young boy but a loner. He learnt quickly from Kagurutsi about animals and bushes, and within a short time he had become quite adept at identifying flora and fauna and their attributes.

Kayibanda was vulgar and harsh towards those who disagreed with his views and opinions. He had perhaps been infected by the vice that had inflicted Rukundakanuzire, his grandfather. This cantankerous demeanour would haunt him throughout his life and it always made people around him fear to oppose or correct him.

One day, Kayibanda drove the cows to the river and found other pastoralists there who had reached there before him. He forced his way to the water source and chased away all the other animals with strokes of his *nkoni* in order for his cows to drink first. That day he was not so lucky, however, and he was beaten until he passed out. When he had fallen into a helpless heap, the pastoralists unzipped their trousers and urinated on him and then walked away.

When Kayibanda regained consciousness, he realised that his head had grown bigger than usual. They had beaten him to pulp with their bare knuckles and damaged his face, and it was all swollen. From that day, he became ruthless and would fight every day with fellow herdsmen. Each time he would be beaten and left with cracked bloody lips and a swollen face. He would lie to his mother and father that he had stumbled and fallen whenever he would be asked what had happened to his face.

Bekunda became pregnant and gave birth to another boy, whom they named Kanyeigabo. Kagurutsi was very happy and so were Kayibanda and Bekunda. Kayibanda was now nine years old and his surrogate father, Kagurutsi, was indeed proud of him. Kagurutsi loved Malanga and had vowed to settle here permanently because his cows had enough water and pasture, unlike where he had wandered about before without settling. He gathered a lot of wood and grass and built a bigger house and kitchen. He also built a granary where he could store the harvests of maize, beans and millet. He and Bekunda and the baby moved into the new hut and left the old one for Kayibanda. Kayibanda was very happy that he now owned a hut of his own, a spear and a machete for protection. He viewed himself as man enough now. He vowed to get up in the middle of the night when everyone was asleep and go hunt down the bastards that had several times beaten him to pulp. He knew where they lived and he planned to sneak there and avenge his beating. The moment he started staying alone in his hut, Kayibanda became a problem in the night. Yet he pretended to be innocent before his parents during the day. He would often be accused of attacking villagers in the night but Kagurutsi would defend him against the allegations. One day Kagurutsi changed into a snake and crawled into Kayibanda's hut and hid under his bed. When Kayibanda calculated that everyone else had slept, he slowly sneaked out to attack his tormentors again.

Kayibanda had earlier tried to attack them several times but they had overpowered and chased him with stones. He had, however, acquired a new tactic. He would take along a burning piece of wood and burn down huts.

Kayibanda followed the footpaths slowly, holding, in one hand, a glowing piece of wood and, in the other, a spear. The snake followed him slowly until Kayibanda reached the compound of a certain man who had many sons. His compound indeed had about twelve huts, evidence that the owner had many children. Kayibanda blew on the burning end of the wood several times and it produced a tongue of flame. He put the fire to the grass that thatched the hut next to which he stood. He choked on smoke and coughed. When he had walked away and stretched out his hand to set fire to another hut, he realised that he had been surrounded. He attempted to run away but was apprehended. In the process Kayibanda managed to hit one boy on the eye with the burning wood. Using water, the crowd put out the fire that had started gutting the huts.

Kagurutsi had been defending his son with passion and hence the child's impunity. Now they had him in their hands and he would not defend him again. The snake watched whatever was taking place in amazement.

The crowd agreed to tie Kayibanda *kandoya* and throw him into the river. They knew that there was no way he would swim through and survive with his arms pulled behind his back and tied to his legs. Kayibanda wailed for forgiveness when they brought ropes and he heard about the planned drowning, but in vain.

Now he started to apologise fervently for all their chickens that he had stolen and roasted and eaten alone while he tended the animals. He apologised for all the cassava and bunches of matooke he had stolen and roasted. They pitied him. The crimes were irreversible now. He was an execrable criminal and now he was in their hands. So they vowed to exterminate him without any excuse. It was at night and no one would know what happened. The next day it would be business as usual. They lifted Kayibanda and took him to the river and threw him in at the deepest end.

The following day, Kayibanda woke up and milked the cows. He didn't know how he came back home and who saved him from drowning. All he remembered was being tied *kandoya* and thrown into the water. He took the cattle to the pasture and kept thinking about the previous night's expedition.

Was I dreaming? he wondered. But he had woken up in the morning in wet clothes and with a cut on the arm. Probably he had been saved by a loving ghost, he thought. 'Oh, hail the loving

Samaritan ghost' he sang and silently laughed at himself. He took the cows to drink water at the river and the boys could not believe what they saw when they cast their eyes on him! He also kept quiet and drove away his cattle when they had finished drinking water. He left them agape.

"This boy must be a ghost. How come he didn't die?" the boy with a protruding tummy asked his brothers.

"We could have killed another boy, thinking that it was Kayibanda," another boy, with tattered shorts, suggested.

"He was Kayibanda. I saw him with my own eyes," another yelled. They were all at a loss for words.

The snake had followed them when they walked down to the river. It had slithered through the reeds and dived into the water when the boys threw Kayibanda into the river. The snake had turned into the human being, Karugutsi, again, and lifted Kayibanda out of the water onto the bank. He had untied him and punched Kayibanda's stomach with his hands and made him throw up the water he had swallowed. Kagurutsi had lifted Kayibanda onto his back and taken him to his hut.

****

One day, Kayibanda woke up early to milk cows. It had rained heavily the previous night. He loathed walking with bare feet in mud mixed with cow dung. He tried to get up and walk out but couldn't. The pain in his feet was excruciating. He couldn't even hold onto the pillar planted into the earth of the hut near the bed for support. Rats had eaten away the soles of both his feet and nibbled the back of four of his fingernails. His hair had been nibbled off too. It was quite a nasty experience. One would easily have mistaken him to be suffering from leprosy. The previous night, they had eaten *eshabwe* and *karo* but he had forgotten to clean himself. He had simply retired peacefully to his bed of papyrus mat, and rats had enjoyed their meal from his unwashed fingers and feet.

He stayed home with Bekunda, who nursed the wounds for about two weeks until his fingers and feet grew back.

Kagurutsi went back to tending the cattle to allow his son to recover.

****

When Kayibanda was around twelve years old, Kagurutsi took him to a school that was several kilometres away. It was in a trading centre. He would wake up every morning, milk the cows, carry the milk on his head and hawk it around the town. Then he would go to school later.

Kayibanda had shown little interest when he was told that he was to start school, he did not know what school meant. A group of missionaries had combed the villages and advised the villagers to send their children to school. Many had understood, but a few had not yet appreciated education. One of the many was Kagurutsi.

One day after selling milk, Kayibanda hid the money inside the cover of one of his books and trudged on to school. He found his classmates already in the classroom doing tests. He stood outside and didn't know what to do next.

The teacher moved out of the classroom and instructed Kayibanda to leave the books outside and join others to do the test. Kayibanda hastily did what he had been instructed to do. He checked where he had kept his money again to be sure it was there and entered class. Immediately after the test, Kayibanda got out briskly, thinking about his money in the book cover. Unfortunately, it was gone! Snorting and taking big strides, he returned to the classroom.

Kayibanda confronted a girl who had stolen a glance at him through the window while he had checked the money before entering the exam room. She denied having stolen the money in front of her fellow pupils and the science teacher. His conscience and premonitions plus the augury experience affirmed to him that she had stolen the money.

Kayibanda remembered how he had got gored by cows earlier in the morning while milking, the countless and hectic movements he had made while selling milk! He lost patience and temper. He slapped the girl on the left buccinator muscle. A coin popped out of her mouth and fell to the ground, drenched in spittle! She suffered public shame as all the class watched with their mouths open.

Kayibanda grew to be a violent boy, a thief and a curmudgeon. His surrogate father, however, did not tire of solving his cases every day. Many people would throng his compound demanding compensation and justice because Kayibanda had beaten their children the previous day or stolen and roasted their chickens. Kagurutsi loved Kayibanda a great deal and pensively planned the next course of action without recrimination.

Often, Kayibanda would be seen cupping stagnant water from the potholes in the road into the can of milk to increase its volume. Kagurutsi came to know about this from his friend Bagarukayo who had caught Kayibanda squatting in the middle of the road scooping the water. Kayibanda had apologised and promised not to do it again, and had begged Bagarukayo never to report him to Kagurutsi.

Kayibanda would wake up in the morning and pretend to be going to school but then wander about the villages stealing people's chickens and selling them cheaply in the nearby town. Then, at dusk, he would walk back home as if he was from school. Kayibanda was a ripe morbid tumour that needed quick piercing with a hot object lest the repercussions and comeuppance would be so unbearable.

Kagurutsi was a quiet man who looked on while incivility unfolded as he brooded over the best way to solve the problems he faced. He looked at violence as a barbarous way to solve problems. He never believed in imposing penance on a person in the name of punishing. He, instead, believed in correction.

Kayibanda was totally different. He always wanted to be a king everywhere he went. He thought that it was the best way to earn respect in society - by forcing everyone to kneel before you. He viewed those who often disagreed with him as enemies and he would find inhuman ways to eliminate them. He was trouble, a rampaging disaster that hit everyone in his way in an effort to satisfy his beliefs. He was like an avalanche of rocks from an eruption rolling down the slopes of the mountain aiming at the valley below. Everyone hated him, at school, in the village and everywhere where he was known.

Kagurutsi sensed that his son would be killed sooner or later. He planned to place him temporarily with a friend, Bamwine, in the farthest district from which he had escaped severe drought before he wandered around the country and finally settled in this village. His friend was also a pastoralist and a chief of Biguri.

"But won't this boy spoil my relationship with Bamwine and we become enemies?" he thought to himself, looking distraught.

"I will talk to Kayibanda while on our way going to Biguri. I believe he will listen to me," he answered himself.

Kayibanda respected Kagurutsi a great deal and listened to him. He would often not repeat a mistake whenever Kagurutsi warned him against it. He would abandon the type of trouble he had caused and instead invent another one. Kayibanda was an inventor of trouble. His father would stop him from doing one thing and he would abandon it and invent another. His creativity in inventing crime was unmatched.

His father invited him one evening for a walk through the tall elephant grass up to the top of a hill. When they arrived there, they sat on a heap of stones. It was dusk and the sky had begun to turn mauve. After they had settled themselves comfortably on the heap of stones, they shared a sugarcane.

"Why have we come here, daddy?" Kayibanda asked, while gazing happily at Kagurutsi.

Kagurutsi heaved a deep sigh and looked into Kayibanda's eyes. His eyes shone, reflecting the dim sunrays that were sinking behind the mountains. He chewed on the sugarcane in his mouth until it was bereft of the juices and spat out the husk. He checked his voice and spoke.

"My son, you have become a disaster in the whole village, school, and the community. Yet at home you give the impression of being a good boy. You are a hypocrite with a very bad demeanour. Why do you not behave well, like other people in the society? Why do you love violence, my son? The other night you went off to burn down people's houses. Had I not followed you, you would have drowned in the river where they threw you. You beat up classmates, you shirk school and prefer to wander about the villages stealing chickens and selling them. You add water to the milk so that you can get money of your own, and so on and so forth. All these things find me here and set me wondering what kind of creature you are. What do you lack, my son? I always provide everything you need but your greed and ego are unquenchable. I want you to tell me today, right now, what the problem is."

Kagurutsi spoke to his son angrily. He was frothing in both corners of his mouth. He was indignant and demanded answers at that very moment. He wiped his mouth with the back of his right hand and bit on his sugarcane. By the time he finished talking, Kayibanda was sweating profusely and his armpit had become wet and he was heaving. He wished to disappear into the earth. He wished he could turn into stones and roll down the slopes of the hill. He had become like an ensnared rat trapped in a snare. He felt shy and had no defence. Everything Kagurutsi had blurted out was the unwavering truth yet he never wanted to admit it.

"What can I do?" he asked himself. It was as if his brain had become divorced from his heart. He had stopped thinking and just stared into space without saying a word.

"Daddy, I am sorry I will not repeat what I've done. Please forgive me. I will be a good son to you from today onwards," Kayibanda said rather contemptuously, gazing at the heap of chewed sugarcane husks. His utterance didn't have an iota of self-reproach. He found it convenient to see his father smile in acquiescence. Deep in his heart, though, Kayibanda wished simply to turn into a hippopotamus and swallow his father so as to do away with shame and future compunction.

Kagurutsi swallowed the juice and spat out the husk. He pitifully looked at his son and couldn't find the words to say to him.

"Listen now. Tomorrow we are going somewhere early in the morning. I am taking you somewhere you will be staying meanwhile as you repair yourself. I have talked to your mother and she is in agreement with me. We shall not accept seeing you here getting wasted and eventually killed. Where I am taking you, it is a long distance from here and we shall spend three days on the way. If you misbehave, Bamwine will take you to prison and you rot there. Agree?" Kagurutsi spoke sternly.

Kayibanda nodded without uttering a word. All the time they had been talking, Kayibanda had not taken a bite on his piece of sugarcane. He held it firmly in his right hand while the left hand held his left cheek as if he was sorrowful.

The following day, Kagurutsi and his son, Kayibanda, started their journey as decided. They took a break from tending animals till he returned. He left the animals in the charge of Bekunda and Kanyeigabo. He had also involved some *juju* to protect the cattle and his family against anything strange that would come to attack them in his absence. They were safe. Kanyeigabo had also started moving with his father and brother to tend the animals. He was growing quickly, and looked as handsome as his father, Kagurutsi. Bekunda loved him with such unmatched intensity that sometimes she felt like she was suffocating. She wished she could give birth to another child - and she would very much have preferred a girl or twins. Kanyeigabo was very inquisitive and he would ask about all sorts of things all the time. Bekunda had quarrelled with Kagurutsi when she weaned off Kanyeigabo without his father's consent. She had reasoned that she wanted to conceive again and he had inquired whether she couldn't do so without weaning off a child.

The distance from home to the road where they would get a bus that would transport them to Mpara town was long. From Mpara, they would walk for a day up to the chief's home in Biguri. He calculated that the journey would take three days. They rustled through the tall grass until they got to the path that connected to the main road. The path wound through a garden of millet. It was too narrow to allow them to walk side by side, so Kayibanda trotted behind Kagurutsi. They didn't talk until they reached the top of a hill and stopped to breakfast on *macunda* and leftovers of *bitakuri* that Bekunda had packed for them.

"Daddy, will you take me to the Bachwezi so that I can also learn the tricks of turning into a lion to defend myself?" Kayibanda asked, while chewing. He swallowed and looked at Kagurutsi as if impatient for a positive answer.

"If you behave well where I am taking you, I shall gift you with a trip to the kingdom where you will be proselytised into the belief. That is where you will be equipped with defensive techniques against enemies aiming at harming you for no good reason," Kagurutsi affirmed.

They finished eating and drinking and journeyed on. It was hot and windy. The sun shone through clear skies, sending down strong rays that burnt them. Perspiration streamed down their cheeks and temples. They needed to be at the bus station before sunset and board the bus that would rumble on the dusty road throughout the night. They increased their pace and eventually reached the bus park when the sun had begun to kiss the mountains. They found many people at the station, also waiting for the bus. They had sacks of food and bags of clothes. They joined them and waited alongside them. Many of the waiting travellers were using their luggage as seats. Kagurutsi and Kayibanda followed suit and sat down on their bags.

Kayibanda sat with his head resting on his knees and arms wrapped around his legs. Before long, he was snoring and Kagurutsi looked on blithely and left him to rest. He knew his son was tired from trudging over such a long distance. The sky was beginning to look mauve from the impending darkness when the white bus showed up at a distance, rumbling on the dusty roads and farting heavy clouds of smoke. It stopped and a scrawny conductor with jeans damaged at the knees and an oversized dirty yellow shirt and tattered canvas shoes jumped out to give instructions. People with light hand luggage were allowed entry first. Among these were Kagurutsi and Kayibanda. They were issued receipts and climbed into the bus. They walked through the aisle searching for a place to sit. Finally, they found two empty seats that were close to the window towards the rear and settled in them. Kayibanda had never travelled in any form of motorised transport before, but he had seen many motor vehicles in the town where he had stayed with the mother before the calamity that her rivals inflicted on her that made them flee the town to seek refuge elsewhere.

The bus roared into life when everyone had entered except three people. These three had more than two bags of charcoal and couldn't be accommodated in the bus. Darkness had started settling when the lumbering bus finished climbing the first hill and began descending towards the valley. Kayibanda had slept off and Kagurutsi had joined some of the other passengers in a conversation.

The bus reached Mpara town when rain was pouring. When the bus stopped in the park, all the passengers remained seated until the rain had reduced to a slight drizzle. There were no taxis to Biguri. Kagurutsi and Kayibanda didn't have any option but to walk yet another long distance that would take them a day. They walked into a restaurant and breakfasted on a heavy meal before continuing through the busy town. They were headed to Biguri road with their bags strapped on their backs.

****

News of Kayibanda's departure was spread through the whole village by Mukamire, Kayibanda's nemesis. He had seen them leave the village through the path that led to the main road. He jumped up and down in happiness and ran through the whole village to disseminate the news. Now was the best time for them to exact revenge since Kagurutsi and his imbecile of a son were not in the village and would seemingly spend days away. Bekunda was alone at home with her son Kanyeigabo. The Bahenda boys thought it a golden chance to set the Kagurutsi homestead on fire and steal the cows and sheep. They planned to attack in the night. The whole day they were in a meeting with Mukamire, assigning responsibilities among themselves. Little did they know that Kagurutsi had left his homestead secure, with spirits of soldiers hovering over the homestead and its precincts.

With Mukamire leading the way, Bahenda's boys walked along the path leading to Kagurutsi's home. They were equipped with a box of matches to set fire to the huts and machetes to slaughter the unwanted cows after they had selected the fat ones to steal and sell. It was a short distance south of their home, conceivably five kilometres across the hill opposite theirs. When they started climbing the hill, under the full moon and in the murky air, they could see Kagurutsi's home, which seemed close by. They walked on and on through the paths.

The spirits were not sleeping, however. The Bachwezi spirits were hovering over Kagurutsi's hill. The spirits descended over the boys and confused them. They lost their way, and eventually turned around and retraced their steps without knowing. They walked into the compound of their home, still influenced by the spirits and divided responsibilities amongst themselves, as had been done earlier in the day. Mukamire was responsible for setting fire to the huts while the five boys were to select the fatty cows and ignore the emaciated ones.

There was a change of programme. They whispered to one another in a hushed meeting behind one hut. They decided they would collectively select the cows and massacre the unwanted ones, and then burn down the huts as they left with the cows. They all agreed to this. They started selecting cows. They selected one hundred of them. Their minds travelled into the future and they could already see themselves rich from the projected sale of the cows. The rest of the cows were treated as scrawny and, therefore, not fit for the market. They slit the throats of all these ones, which numbered two hundred. They drove the healthy one hundred cows up to the valley and returned to burn the huts. When they stepped in the compound ready to set the huts on fire, the spirits lifted off and they realised that they were at their own home. They wailed angrily, not over the foiled plan to gut Kagurutsi's home and massacre his cattle but over the fact that the onslaught against their own home and cattle had been carried out by themselves. They wondered what had infiltrated their souls and caused them to do such a thing to their own cows. The wailing was loud enough to wake up Bahenda. He couldn't believe it when he was welcomed by the river of blood that flowed from the kraal into the compound.

The boys turned against Mukamire, viewing him as having conspired to confuse them and make Bahenda's family poor. One of the boys cut off Mukamire's head before he could open his mouth to defend himself. Bahenda collapsed and died upon seeing what his sons had done. After learning about the death of his son, Mukamire's father, together with his other sons, ransacked Bahenda's home the following day and finished off Bahenda's two sons, set the home on fire and took away the one hundred cows together with his son's corpse.

Kayibanda was excited when they entered Chief Bamwine's compound. It was like a paradise. They were all tired and hungry and dirty from the long journey on the dusty road from Mpara town to Biguri village. Darkness had started settling in when they reached the chief's home. They met the chief in the compound doing postprandial exercise. Chief was a plump man with a protruding belly and a bald, shiny head. He stopped jogging and tried to examine the uninvited visitors from a misty distance.

"Chief, sorry we have bombarded your home uninvited, but please forgive us. This is my son Kayibanda. I have brought him here to be your servant while attending school. He has been in Primary Four," Kagurutsi said apologetically.

"Oh my long-lost friend Kagurutsi, how have you been? Long time and I am happy to see you this evening," the chief said, smiling from ear to ear.

He got closer, opened out his arms and gathered them into a hug.

"You have grown scrawny. The condition there is not yet good where you are wandering about? Please come back here. The cows you left me with have multiplied and they are now over one hundred. The climate is okay here," the chief said, while releasing them. "Come on, let's get into the house." The chief led the way into the house.

When Kagurutsi had left Biguri, there were no iron-roofed houses there. But this time he had seen two or three and the biggest one was Chief Bamwine's. Through the back door they were led to the boy's quarters, where Bamwine showed them a room where they would stay. After bathing and changing into clothes they had bought in Mpara town, Kagurutsi and Kayibanda returned to the big house where they found the rest of the Bamwine family. They ate supper and went to bed except Bamwine and Kagurutsi, who talked throughout the night.

The chief had three daughters and two sons and they were both in school. They commuted from home every day and were happy to be joined by Kayibanda. Kagurutsi promised Bamwine that he would be coming back to the village. He pleaded with Bamwine to imbue his son with knowledge and wisdom.

Kayibanda looked at Bamwine's daughters and his mind sped into the future. He saw himself marrying one. The girls were very beautiful; it was as though they had fallen from Mars. For a few minutes he had been lost in thought while his eyes were fixed on Kabandize. She was the older girl, and was raking the compound, heaping the fallen leaves under the tree. Kayibanda's father pinched him and advised him to behave. Kayibanda's mind reverted to real life and he promised to be a good boy.

Kagurutsi spent three days with them and left when Bamwine had secured a place for Kayibanda at the nearby school where his children had been studying. Kayibanda quickly got acclimated to the community and he was liked by everyone in the village. This was not because he was handsome or intelligent or gregarious but because he was a polyglot, and he boasted about it. He spoke French, Kinyarwanda, some broken English, and Runyankore. His peers wondered how he had mastered those languages at his age. If only they knew the journey of his life up to where he was now! He was a loner and many desired his company but all in vain, except for his new brothers and sisters in Chief Bamwine's family.

Kayibanda's best friend was Kabandize. Kayibanda was very poor at academics, sports and other curricular activities. All he did was boast about how he came from the rich family of the famous Chief Bamwine. He had quickly forgotten the agreement he had made with Kagurutsi. He had now graduated from poverty and squalor and joined the royals. He had switched from being violent and stealing chickens and now found a new trade in boasting around. He always invented something nasty to do after abandoning the other. He was a boy to whom memories were an encumbrance rather than a lesson.

On his way to Mpara town, Kagurutsi turned off into the bush and clambered his way up to the top of a rock outcrop to thank the Bachwezi spirits for the protection they had afforded him. It had been long since he last came to this sacred rock to speak with the spirits. He removed the *rugabire* from his feet and sat down on the rock like a Chinese monk. He started uttering incantations, thanking the Bachwezi for protecting his family from trouble while he was away. He also prayed for his sons and wife and finally asked the gods for more powers. Then he left to catch a bus in Mpara town. He was a man with an unwavering devotion to what he believed in.

Barungi, Bamwine's wife, was busy winnowing beans on a howling windy sunny day while Kayibanda and Kabandize were playing, capering about on a heap of chaff as she blithely watched them over yonder. She cupped her hands around the chaff-less legumes, scooped them up into the woven old basket some more times until it was full to the brim. Then she yelled at Kayibanda, brandishing her flabby arms, to hurry and lift the shapeless basket to the grass-thatched granary that stood askew a stone's throw away from where they were playing.

Kayibanda frantically looked at her. He hated the grubby apron she wore, splattered with banana sap and blood stains from the previous day's chicken slaughter. He covered the disgruntled look on his face with both hands and hastily moved towards where she had placed the basket full of beans. He lifted it up onto the shoulder and some few seeds spilt. He lumbered to the grass-thatched granary, ducked his head into the tiny lone window, lowered the basket inside, poured the beans and took the basket back to Barungi for refilling. Bamwine was so industrious, he had a forest of coffee that covered almost the whole hill, a large herd of cattle and flock of sheep, and acres of bananas, potatoes and other food crops.

The sky was beginning to turn mauve when Barungi finished filling the last basket. The huge basket was polished with cow dung on the outside perhaps to fill in the holes that could let out beans or grains of millet.

She yelled at Kayibanda again, forlornly thrusting herself to her feet, to come quickly and ferry some more beans to the granary. To her disappointment, Kayibanda didn't answer. He and Kabandize had got stuck in a gumboot as they played. Bamwine's gumboots. They had argued about who was meant to wear the remaining boot after Kayibanda had pulled on the first one. So in the skirmish they both slid their feet into the one boot. Unfortunately, they couldn't get out their feet by themselves, so they sat there silently and shed tears.

When Barungi turned to see what the matter was and established what had happened, she hurriedly tried to get their feet out by pulling on their legs. Her efforts were fruitless. It was only until the chief came that the feet were eventually got out. The chief had to forfeit his only pair of boots in the process. Both children had smudges on their ankles and Barungi helped to treat them before the bruises could turn into wounds.

One day, the bell for games rang and all the children jumped out of the class and thronged the school compound to play. Some went to sweep their classes and others went to the playground to play football. Kayibanda followed a group of girls who went through the forest to the dam to swim. His aim was to see them undress and to drool at their nakedness. He was fond of that. He would lurk around the forest and his eyes would be glued to the dam whenever the girls swam.

There was a girl Kayibanda was crazy about but that had turned him down. So he had vowed to punish her one day. When the girls had reached the dam and all had undressed, Kayibanda leered at them from his hideout among the shrubs nearby like a hyena. He examined all their features and noticed the differences in their hips, buttocks and the plums protruding on their chests. The girls laughed at Akunda because she was the only girl with small plums on the chest; others had bigger ones. And yet Akunda was the one whom Kayibanda had a crush on. His love for her was immoderate and unmatched.

The girls dived into the dam and swam happily. While they were busy enjoying themselves in the water, Kayibanda crawled to the bank of the dam where the girls had heaped their clothes. He stole Akunda's uniform and crawled back into the shrubs where he gathered himself up and ran away. The bell rang for the assembly and the scattered children gathered and lined up according to their classes and heights. The girls who had been swimming in the pond got out hurriedly, too, and dressed up. However, Akunda couldn't find her uniform. The girls ran and joined others at the assembly. Akunda, too, ran behind them and joined the assemblage with her hands covering her little plums on the chest. Everyone turned and all the eyes rested on the stoical Akunda.

"Where is your uniform Akunda?" the senior woman asked with concern.

"I don't know who has stolen it, madam," Akunda replied with fear.

"Teacher, Kayibanda has Akunda's uniform hidden in his bag," one pupil who had indeed seen Kayibanda said. "I saw him hiding it in his bag."

Indeed Kayibanda's bag was protruding. And when it was opened, Akunda's uniform was seen stuck there, folded. The following day Kayibanda was bundled into a pick-up with his belongings and taken to a boarding school in Mpara town, where Chief Bamwine instructed the school authorities to watch him closely and never allow him out. Bamwine was very furious about Kayibanda's uncouth behaviour. He wondered what sort of human his long-time friend and fellow pastoralist had brought him.

Kayibanda was remorseful about what he had done. He begged the chief for forgiveness. The chief administered thirty strokes of the cane to his buttock. The upshot was that when he reached the new school his buttocks were swollen and he promised never to misbehave again. Now it seemed Kayibanda had run out of new vices. He tried all the uncouth things but couldn't repeat what he had done before. He had to go back to the drawing board and search for new ones. He thought he was unlucky because every vice he invented saw him heavily punished.

When the term ended, Chief Bamwine went to Kayibanda's school to pick him up. To his disappointment, Kayibanda was waiting to be picked up without anything except the clothes he wore and shoes of different sizes and fashion. The suitcase he had come with to school had no lid and in it were only a few sheets of paper. The mattress, blanket, and bed sheets had all been stolen. Bamwine was furious. When they reached home, Kayibanda was ordered to uproot all the unwanted grass and thorny trees from the farm.

One day, Kayibanda thought of carrying some embers from home to the farm where he worked so that he could roast some matooke or potatoes. While he stealthily carried the coals on a potsherd to the farm, hobbling because of the ache in his foot, some fell in the dry grass but he didn't notice it. Within three minutes, part of the farm was burning and the fire, driven by a howling wind, was greedily mauling away at the dry grass. If it hadn't been for the intervention of a third force, the whole village would have been burnt down.

That holiday, Kayibanda worked like a donkey until he finished cleaning the farm as he had been instructed. Evening milking would be done early before sunset and all the milk would be kept for home consumption. This was unlike in the morning, when Bamwine would sell the milk to a certain plump man whose name was long and difficult to pronounce – in order to do so, one needed to gather all the breath in one's chest and pour it out as though spurting out a hot potato or vomit. He had a huge wide-open nose, blubbery mouth and bald head. He would come as early as 7.00 am and measure the milk with Kayibanda, pour it into huge stainless steel cans, load them into his vehicle and drive away, disappearing into the morning mist.

Among Bamwine's cows was a stubborn brown one with wide horns which Kayibanda had nicknamed *'Ntandali'*. While other cows would be munching on the grass, it would be standing and chewing the cud nonchalantly. The moment it realised that you were no longer looking at it, it would disappear through the hedges that formed the boundaries between the farm and the neighbouring gardens and start chewing away at food crops. It was very difficult to milk it. It would jump and gore at Kayibanda all the time, and then it would run and hide in the shrubs for its calf to enjoy the milk to the maximum.

A few litres of the milk would be reserved for dogs and a pussy cat. Kayibanda's role after school was to look after the calves and sheep in a stretch of paddock near home that had scattered trees which he could use as shelter from a downpour and the scorching sun. Bamwine knew that Kayibanda was indefatigable, so he would assign him hectic duties at home, perhaps to nurture him and get him to cultivate a strong work ethic and a sense of responsibility at an early stage. Bamwine love for the pipe nauseated Kayibanda because of the unpleasant smell that frequently wafted into his nostrils, but, with time, the boy got used to his ways and enjoyed the moments with him.

When the holiday ended, Chief Bamwine sold off some of the cows belonging to Kagurutsi and went with Kayibanda to the local market to buy a few things for Kayibanda to return to school with. It was a very cold morning in Biguri because it had rained throughout the night and the sun was ineffectual. Kayibanda shivered and shoved both his hands in the pockets of his shorts. A school bag was strapped to his back and he silently walked behind Chief Bamwine.

Kayibanda had only two hundred shillings in his pocket. Part of that money was supposed to pay Kayibanda's fees, part of it was for shopping at the market and part was their transport. After they had finished shopping in Mpara town, Chief Bamwine reminded Kayibanda that it was getting late and so they should proceed to the taxi park and take a taxi to the school. As they trudged on through the market, Kayibanda stumbled on a jutting stone and fell on his knees because he couldn't cope with the chief's giant strides. The chief hurled insults at him and reminded him to look where he was going. As Kayibanda gathered the strength to collect himself and get back on his feet again, his shorts ruptured and his genitals peeped out. Opposite where he knelt was a woman, bent facing the other way. She was busy rummaging through a heap of *mivumba* clothes. Kayibanda looked closely as the wind blew her loose dress. The lady watched between her legs and also saw what had had happened to Kayibanda's shorts and what had followed.

Chief Bamwine noticed the drama between Kayibanda and the mysterious woman. He rolled his right hand into a fist and hit Kayibanda hard on his clean-shaven head, and got hold of his hand before they briskly moved on.

It was when his organs popped out that Kayibanda realised he had no underwear. "We have not bought the underwear and my shorts have ruptured," he grumbled.

They went back to the market to look for one or two pairs of underwear. They moved to and fro among several stalls. Bamwine had insisted on paying five shillings for a pair of good cotton underwear but the trader's last price was ten shillings.

"Give me the money," Kayibanda suggested. "I will buy the underwear myself at a town near the school."

"You have never worn pajamas. Why are you bothered about them now?" Bamwine snorted, before adding in a harsh tone, "You will start wearing underwear when you reach Senior One."

They left the market without underwear. They reached the school by seven o'clock and marched direct to the headmaster's office. At the office, Kayibanda received a stern warning from Bamwine that, should he blunder again, he should not return home at the end of the term.

Kayibanda was now stuck with an impotent mind that no longer had the ability to manufacture new vices. The only bad habits that had never earned him punishment were perhaps boasting around fellow students and bearing ill-will towards those who held divergent views from his. He had a habit of sneering at those who disagreed with him and wishing that thunder could strike them dead so that he could be surrounded by only those who agreed with him. He blamed everyone else for the bad things that happened around him and credited only himself for the good things.

Kayibanda loved reading materials irrelevant to the subjects taught at school. For example, he would be found reading William Shakespeare while in primary school, and, while in secondary school, he would be reading about communism and capitalism. This led to his poor performance at primary, secondary and high school levels. Of course, he was sharpening his intellectual acuity to always take part in mature arguments since he liked bragging around like someone who knew everything about everything. He was a follower of politics, and, after his high school, he was recruited into the internal security organisation as a spy to carry out espionage on those opposing the colonial government. He would later be given a full sponsorship to study at a university abroad. However, because of his low intelligence, he abandoned the course he had been given at the university and returned to his home country to continue working for the colonial government.

****

During one of his Senior Four vacations, Kayibanda travelled to Malanga village to spend time with his family. He had last seen them the day his father had brought him to stay with Chief Bamwine several years before. Now he was a young man of about twenty-six and he had already grown a beard and a moustache. He was not sure whether Kagurutsi or Bekunda or Kanyeigabo would recognize him since they had last seen him when he was a toddler. Bamwine had done an excellent job of educating Kayibanda up to secondary school level. He was proud of him, just as he was proud of his sons and daughters. Chief Bamwine went with Kayibanda to Mpara town where he bought packets of sugar and bars of soap and saw him off at the bus station. At that time, there were no means of communication such as phones, so Kayibanda would just show up at home without first sending out word about his impending visit. In Malanga village, Kayibanda had made a lot of foes before he was taken to stay at Chief Bamwine's home. He now wished he could find these foes there and reconcile with them since he was no longer a villager like them. The roads were now fine and it took the bus only a few hours to reach Mpuma where it stopped and he alighted. Indeed, the area was developing speedily. At the stage he found men with bicycles to hire for a ride to Malanga village at a small fare. Kayibanda sat on the carrier of one bicycle with his huge bag strapped to his back while the small one was slung on his shoulder. The cyclist - tall, bearded and with a dark complexion - sat comfortably on the saddle and peddled the bicycle into motion. They crept down the hill to the valley in silence. When they reached the bottom of the hill, the rider got off and Kayibanda did so, too.

The cyclist pushed the bicycle up to the top of the hill and they sat on the bike again and rode again until they reached Malanga village. He stopped at a junction in the middle of the sorghum garden where there was a labyrinth of different paths that disappeared into the garden.

"Where, in Malanga, are you going, sir? What home?" the rider asked in a husky voice while panting for breath.

The sun had sunk behind the mountains but darkness had not yet descended on the village. However, because of the tall stalks of sorghum, it appeared as though darkness had started falling.

"Kagurutsi's home. I am his son, Kayibanda," Kayibanda replied as he examined the rider's face, which seemed familiar.

"Oh! Haya, let's move on," the rider said and peddled on. He stopped at a distance and asked Kayibanda to get off the bicycle and walk home. The rider refused to reach the home where Kayibanda was going, and Kayibanda wondered why. Kayibanda reached into his pocket, paid the rider and told him to keep the change. He walked away bouncing as if he had springs on his shoe heels.

"This brute has come back to the village! Okay! We still hold the pain you inflicted on us in in our hearts. Do not think that your departure left us in a happy state," the rider cursed under his breath as he watched Kayibanda bounce on the path, through the long grass to his home.

He peddled off and disappeared into the mist. He was Bahenda's son. When he reached home, he shared the news of

Kayibanda's return with his brothers. They were sad, not because of his coming back but because of the memories that flashed through their minds. They had vowed never to revenge again. The night they had stupidly chosen to revenge, the comeuppance had been regrettable.

But again they plotted how to punish the bastard. They agreed to ambush and castrate him when he was alone on his way to the bus stage to catch a bus to return to wherever he had been staying.

When Kayibanda set foot in the compound, he found his mother preparing *emikaro*. She was seated on an animal skin in the compound. Bekunda watched a smart man get close to where she sat and she stopped what she was doing. She almost ran mad when she noticed that the man was her son! It had been long, but still she couldn't forget her son, her beloved son. She hurriedly rose from where she was seated and flew across the remaining distance between them. With loud ululations, Bekunda hugged Kayibanda tightly and 'accused' him of over-growing.

"It seems where you are you do not do anything," she wondered happily as she seized his small bag from his shoulders.

Kayibanda also noticed that her mother had grown at an indescribable speed. She had grown thick and coarse, and wrinkles had developed on her face and neck, and her hair had been cut short, starting to grey. She was a caricature of what she had been years before when he left Malanga village.

Kayibanda put the bag down on the carpet of grass and sat on a bench. Bekunda walked quickly into the house and returned with a gourd of *macunda*. She handed it to Kayibanda, who put it to his mouth and gulped down the contents as if he had not eaten in days. He put the gourd down when he had finished and cleaned the whitish smudge on the mouth with the back of his hand.

"Thank you, Mum, it has been really long since I last enjoyed something prepared by you," Kayibanda said as he belched.

He rose and walked towards the house with his bags in both hands. He disappeared into the house for a few minutes and came out again.

"Where are Dad and Kanyeigabo?" Kayibanda asked, standing at the threshold of the house while facing the compound where his mum sat finishing up what she was doing. "Daddy is still in the fields tending the cattle while Kanyeigabo has gone to fetch water from the river," Bekunda said as she gathered herself up, picked up the bowl and entered the kitchen.

Meanwhile, Kayibanda walked towards the rack. He started washing the utensils in a big saucepan and putting them up on the upper rack.

"No, do not do that," Bekunda yelled at him as he tried to scrub a saucepan which they had used to cook *karo*. The saucepan had been placed somewhere under the shed and filled with water to ease cleaning.

"What do you want me to do, Mom?" Kayibanda shot back, confused.

"Go and sit there on the bench under the tree. I am bringing you your favourite food," she answered.

Kanyeigabo returned from the river carrying a jerrican of water on his head. Kayibanda stepped forward to help him put it down. Soon, they were conjoined in hugs and greetings. Kagurutsi, too, had come and joined in. The whole family was happy about the reunion with Kayibanda, who had spent many years away. They ate supper under the full moon and in cool breeze. When they had finished, Kayibanda walked into the house and came out with the bigger bag. He gave everyone gifts he had bought for them and finally the groceries that Chief Bamwine had bought for the family. They were all very happy and went to bed.

The following day was a Sunday and Kayibanda delayed waking up. He was very tired from the long journey. Sunrays that stole into his hut through the tiny openings in the window had fallen direct onto his uncovered face on a bed made of papyrus. Kagurutsi and Kanyeigabo had gone to tend the animals while Bekunda was outside scrubbing saucepans. The noise of the sand being rubbed against the insides of saucepans in cleaning was enough to drive Kayibanda from bed.

Whilee he was rummaging through the bag for what to wear, he heard someone stepping into the compound and greeting his mother. Soon after, he heard his mom exchanging pleasantries with some girl whom he didn't recognise at first. Later, however, he peeped through a chink in the door of his hut and saw a now grown-up Kembaga who had been his girlfriend when he left Malanga village. She had heard the rumour that his boyfriend had come back from school. Kembaga asked Bekunda where Kayibanda was but Bekunda lied that Kayibanda was not around.

"Iyiiiii, but my brother and sister saw him pass by our home yesterday in the evening," the girl protested, her face flooded with love. She was very disappointed at Bekunda's utterance of lies.

"I told you he is not here. Don't you listen, young girl?" Bekunda blurted out, furious. She picked up a piece of wood to hit her. Kembaga turned with haste and ran away without looking back.

"This fool of a woman doesn't know that I am her daughter-in-law. If she knew how much Kayibanda loves me, she would even be respecting me. I hate you, fool! I wish you die tomorrow so that by the time I marry your son, your grave will be choking with a forest of weed on top," Kembaga said, tears rolling down the cheeks. "I am going to bewitch him so that he loves only me. I swear to Kazooba Nyamuhanga that Kayibanda's penis will only erect for me, not any other woman in this world. I will go to Nyamwezi tomorrow and see the *murangi*."

Kayibanda hastily dressed up and pushed the door open with his foot while he buttoned his shirt and got out to see the girl, but she had gone. He marched to the kitchen and stood in the doorway while fastening his trouser belt.

"Mom, why did you lie?" Kayibanda asked his mother, furious. She was busy tasting *eshabwe* which she had dropped on her palm to ascertain whether it had enough salt.

"I do not want these village girls to spoil my son. Keep busy with your books and no one should disturb you," she said angrily, stirring in the bowl of *eshabwe* without raising her head.

Kayibanda couldn't understand her mother's intention in hoarding him like a miser's money. He didn't know that she wanted him to associate only with people of his caliber, not village rejects and loafers like Kembaga. Little did Bekunda know that she was ridiculing and throwing tirades at her future daughter-in-law, Kembaga.

Kagurutsi was a very generous man; an open-handed, lavish giver. No matter who turned up in his compound, he would share the only meal in the kitchen with them. And Bekunda would have the hectic task of cooking another meal for the family members.

One evening at dusk, while Kayibanda locked the calves inside their byres that stood askew near the kraal, Kagurutsi was watching him as he listened to news on the radio. A couple were trudging by along the path near the Kagurutsi home from the market. They were headed back to their village with their luggage strapped to their backs like babies. Kagurutsi looked at the tired couple with pity and sympathy as they strode on tirelessly. He invited them home to eat something before they could continue with their journey. He was not sure whether food was available yet he confidently invited the passers-by. Kayibanda looked at his father in bewilderment because he knew that his mother had just put water on fire to boil for cooking *karo.*

The couple happily turned into the compound and greeted Kagurutsi excitedly. They expressed wonder about how he knew about their gut-gnawing hunger and thirst. Their faces registered joy and excitement.

Kayibanda examined them as he greeted them and ushered them to the visitors' bench under the mango tree that stood firmly in the middle of the compound. The mango tree had a mass of glossy leaves and beautiful flowers that often attracted a swarm of bees and other pollen-collecting insects when it flowered. Kayibanda watched Bekunda dip the gourd into a pot of *bushera* that sat snugly in the corner of the kitchen. She got out and served the visitors happily as though she had been expecting them. After they had finished drinking, they ate ravenously, and proceeded to bless Kagurutsi effusively. Then they got up and disappeared into the darkness. From what they said, they still had a long way to go, they had brought goats to sell at Malanga market that took place every first day of the month. Kayibanda pitied them as they disappeared into the darkness. He wondered why they couldn't use a portion of the proceeds from the sales they had made to travel by taxi.

Kagurutsi could read his son's baffled face. He told him that they moved long distances to sell goats in order to raise money to educate their children or build good houses. It is then that Kayibanda remembered that the following week was the beginning of the New Year and that he had been admitted to high school. They had listened to the announcements on radio.

Although Bekunda didn't want her son to get involved with ladies yet, Kayibanda was very promiscuous at school and in Biguri village. After his mother had chased away Kembaga, Kayibanda had gone to their home and apologised to her for the incident. Kayibanda had moved with her to the nearby trading centre where they treated themselves to Fanta and Marie tea biscuits. She was very happy that, finally, her man had come back. Kembaga's father was also a pastoralist who had settled in Malanga many years before. She was in Primary Six and had repeated it two times. Kayibanda loved Kembaga because she was a very beautiful woman with a voluptuous figure and big, sparkling eyes like the headlamps of a new car. She was indeed the daughter of a pastoralist. During the whole holiday, Kayibanda met Kembaga three times every week. They would meet at the trading centre or at the river or on top of a hill where they would enjoy each other's warmth and lips.

One night Kayibanda was returning from guzzling some beers at the trading centre when he suddenly ran into a very beautiful young woman of his own age. Kenkwanzi, as she introduced herself when Kayibanda approached her, even spoke English very well. The moon was still young in the sky, which sparkled with innumerable stars, but Kayibanda was able to examine the young woman very well. Kenkwanzi was very beautiful. Comparing her to Kembaga was like comparing a cat to a pig.

Kayibanda was struck by Kenkwanzi's indescribable beauty and presentation. They sat in the grass near the road and talked a great deal, mostly about themselves and their plans after education. Kayibanda realised that he was deeply in love with Kenkwanzi. At that moment, Kembaga and all the uncountable women he had seen before appeared absolutely unremarkable. Kayibanda proposed marriage to Kenkwanzi. She was very excited and smiled from ear to ear, exposing her sparkling white, evenly spaced teeth and the big gap in her upper front teeth. Her skin was very smooth and light. She had long, lush hair that fell on her shoulders. She agreed but insisted that Kayibanda should visit their home the next day. She gave him directions to their home.

When they stood up to go, Kayibanda opened his arms and gathered her into a hug and kissed her on the lips. He felt that he had found love and concluded that the other ladies were just wasting his time. The feeling was mutual and Kenkwanzi expressed that she had never before met a loving man like him. He suggested that he escorts her up to their compound. However, she turned down the offer. They said bye to each other and parted ways, promising to meet the following day.

The following day it rained heavily and non-stop. Kayibanda was furious at the heavy rain and wished it would stop so that he could go to meet the love of his life. He had not at all thought about Kembaga. All his thoughts were now focused on Kenkwanzi, the most beautiful woman in the world. He kept thinking and smiling to himself. What he had felt the previous night came back to him - his hands massaging her succulent erect breasts, the slim waistline and the satiny thighs. Her soft lips, velvety fingers and sharp, long nose almost drove Kayibanda crazy. He wished for a car to drive in the downpour to her place.

When the rain stopped pouring, it started drizzling. Kayibanda got out of his hut and walked in the slight drizzle with a jacket covering his head. He hurried, his feet rustling through the wet grass. However, the torrent resumed. Kayibanda vowed not to return home and found shelter under a big jackfruit tree. He was very impatient to meet Kenkwanzi. He thought that he was delaying her and that she was mad at his delay in reaching her parents' home. When it finally stopped raining, the legs of his jeans were wet up to the knees and the sneakers were dripping with water. In a few minutes, he was at the address which Kenkwanzi had said was their place. He was warmly welcomed by a woman who looked exactly like Kenkwanzi. Now he had no doubt and didn't need to ask whether he was in the right place. Kayibanda was ushered into the house and served food and milk.

"So, where do you come from and what brings you here, young man of my last boy's age?" the middle-aged woman asked curiously and proceeded to examine Kayibanda's face. Then she smiled and took a bite on the food.

"I am Kayibanda, son of Kagurutsi from Malanga and I have come to visit Kenkwanzi. We were together at Mweru trading centre last night and she is the one who directed me here. I promised to visit her without fail today and here I am!" Kayibanda asserted.

"What? You saw Kenkwanzi last night? Ehhh, my son, you saw the wrong person. Kenkwanzi died three years ago. That's her grave over there in the compound," the woman said. She looked terribly surprised as she pointed at the grave which was visible through the door.

Kayibanda protested at the woman's announcement. He almost jumped out of the house with fear. The woman walked to the lampstand and returned with a picture of Kenkwanzi. She handed it to Kayibanda and asked him to examine and confirm whether she was the one. He held it up and indeed confirmed she was the one. Kayibanda admitted that he had been with Kenkwanzi's ghost. The woman looked at the young man with sympathetic eyes and advised him to forget about her daughter and go back home.

Kenkwanzi's mother had received many men at her home and they had all come alleging that her daughter had directed them there. Kenkwanzi had committed suicide after her mother had refused her to get married to the man she madly loved. She had left a note on her bed asking her mother never to tire of receiving her visitors.

On his way back home, Kayibanda developed diarrhoea because of the shocking revelation. He had to go into the bush several times to relieve himself. And when he reached home, he rushed straight into the latrine. When he entered the latrine and pulled down his trousers, ready to squat over the hole, a voice he recognised as Kenkwanzi's squealed: "Do not sit on me please, my love Kayibanda."

He jumped out of the latrine and the diarrhoea immediately disappeared. He ran through the compound into his hut. He banged the door shut behind him and looked towards his bed only to see that the beautiful Kenkwanzi sat on it! She was naked and her legs were crossed. She was smiling.

"You said you love me. Now why you are scared of me, baby? I am here for you now. Join me on this bed and we make love,"

Kenkwanzi coaxed. She then proceeded to threaten to strangle him if he refused or raised an alarm.

Kayibanda was now sweating profusely and every pore on his body oozed sweat. He wished he could turn into a crocodile and swallow up this ghost. However, this was impossible. He wished to disappear into the earth, but all in vain. The ghost stretched its arm as though it was elastic and reached for Kayibanda, who still stood dumbstruck and transfixed near the door. Soon, they were on the bed, conjoined. Kayibanda was later taken for exorcism at a *murangi*'s shrine in the next village and warned never again to talk to any beautiful woman he ran into on the road at night. He had learnt the hard way and vowed to beat up any lady he found walking alone in the night.

****

When Kayibanda was returning to Biguri the following day, he met Kembaga. They strolled together through the village path and sat on top of a certain hill, on a heap of stones where Kayibanda and Kagurutsi had sat many years before and eaten sugarcane. It was dark. Kayibanda told Kembaga that he was going back to school the following day. Kembaga cried and begged to go with him so that they could start life together. Kayibanda urged her to be patient with him as he finished his studies. He would then get a job and pick her up so that they could live together. She reached for his lips and passed hers on his. Soon they were all aroused and intertwined on the carpet of grass.

When Kayibanda joined high school, Chief Bamwine saw

no reason to continue tiring himself escorting Kayibanda to school, like a nursery school child. After all, he had improved in manners.

When he got to Senior Five, Kayibanda was given fees and sent off to school in Mpara town. He was not, however, given pocket money. He didn't know how he would survive with his many girlfriends in school. During the first week of the term, Kayibanda was not at school. He had taken his case to the home of one of his friends, who lived in a certain slum in Mpara town, and kept it there.

Kayibanda decided to use the school fees he had been given to make a profit. He went to the villages and bought three cows cheaply and took them to the market, where he was paid handsomely. Now he had doubled his money. He wanted more. He again went to the villages and bought seven other cows cheaply and sold them before he could even reach the market.

Kayibanda didn't see the value of education when he could make money so quickly. He kept selling cows and made huge profits each time. On one Sunday, he picked up his case and reported to school, where he had planned he would become a usurer to students and even teachers. He now viewed himself as a magnate.

The usury business went on very well.

When the holidays came around, he wrote to Chief Bamwine to tell him that he would not come to his palace for the holidays and listed a number of reasons in the letter.

Kayibanda rented a *muzigo* in Mpara town and concentrated on selling cows. He would go to the villages, buy them cheaply and bring them to the market where he would make profits. He would have acquired wealth quickly if he had invested the profits in a certain business, but his penchant for women and splurging on unproductive things ensured that this didn't happen. What he kept untouched was only capital and perhaps the fees.

When the year began, Kayibanda, who was now in Senior Six, paid his *muzigo* rent for the whole year so that the property in the tenement room was secure. He would start from there after leaving school. He reported back to school early because an announcement was aired on radio that tests were to be written in the first week of reporting. Kayibanda had chosen to read history, geography and economics. He banked half of the money he had made, and went with the other half to school. He intended to use part of the money to pay fees and survive on the remainder as pocket money. He would perhaps invest part of the money in his secret money lending business. He was a tycoon at school and everyone wished to associate with him because of his money.

One visiting day at Kayibanda's school, he woke up and laid his bed, bathed and went to the school dining hall for breakfast. The dining hall was half a kilometre away from the dormitories. Teacher Moses, as he was known, caught Kayibanda going to the kitchen with a china cup, unlike the other students, who carried uniform plastic blue cups. He led him to the staffroom and ordered that he should get reeds and fix the urinals as a punishment for breaking school rules. He handed Kayibanda a machete and directed him where to cut the reeds. He allowed him only thirty minutes to finish the punishment.

Moses was the teacher on duty, so Kayibanda heeded his order because he didn't want trouble. Indeed, after thirty minutes the teacher came to inspect what Kayibanda had done and whether he had finished the punishment. Kayibanda was inside the reed-urinals as Moses was busy inspecting and scrutinising what the boy had done from the outside. Kayibanda unzipped his shorts and, holding his organ in his hand, positioned it properly, showering Teacher Moses with a rapid spring of urine and sniggering.

Teacher Moses initially thought it had started raining, then wondered why the raindrops would be warm and smelly. He cursed, and bitter sobs escaped from his throat. He immediately vowed to expel Kayibanda forthwith.

When Teacher Moses confronted Kayibanda, the latter retorted: "Remember we drink together at the *kafunda* every night." Kayibanda reminded Teacher Moses that he had caught him red-handed behind the door of one classroom with his girlfriend, a student of that same school, during prep the previous week. "You will be ashamed to expel me for piddling on you while I 'inaugurated' what I had been renovating," Kayibanda sniggered.

Kayibanda and Teacher Moses reached a consensus that that night Kayibanda would buy beer at the kafunda as a gesture of repentance. That night, it rained heavily and Kayibanda didn't show up at the bar.

Teacher Moses never confronted Kayibanda again until he left the school. Bamwine did not even show up on the visiting day despite the numerous radio announcements about the occasion.

Kayibanda was even worried that the chief would find him serving the punishment. He kept peeping over the hedges to see whether he would be seen entering the gate. Ever since he had written to him informing him that he would not be going home for the holiday, Bamwine had not replied. 'Perhaps he was furious at my decision?' he had asked himself.

Kayibanda was expelled from school when the second term had just begun. He had been found kissing Kamagoba, one of his girlfriends. Teacher Bashisha had been moving about the library and had seen, through the book shelves, a boy's head and that of a girl coming together and conjoining into a passionate kiss. The two culprits were summoned into the staffroom and the headmaster issued both with expulsion letters. He advised them to come to the school only to write their exams. He instructed that they should be escorted by police officers and that they should only be allowed to sit after completing their fees and paying fines.

Kayibanda was both happy and sad. He was happy that he had got time off school to make more money; and he was sad that some of the students that he had lent money had not yet paid back. He knew that some of the students were insolvent, and he wasn't sure whether they would ever clear their debts. Both Kayibanda and his girlfriend were given five minutes to pack up and disappear from the school compound. Kayibanda was led to the dormitories to pack his belongings. He picked up his mattress and case and went out of the gate, where he met Kamagoba crying loudly like a starved baby that needs to suckle.

"My ffffaather ww-willl kill me. I don't want to go home,"

Kamagoba told Kayibanda. She looked so sad, and tears ran down her cheeks.

"Come on, let's go to Mpara town and talk over lunch on the way forward," Kayibanda suggested while holding her hand.

They reached Tourist Hotel in Mpara town and sat on the restaurant side, huddled in a corner and facing each other. Kamagoba was a beautiful girl with a huge behind. She was, however, quite short. Kayibanda was involved with her just for the fun of it; he really was not in love with her. They talked over lunch of *matooke* and groundnut sauce. She expressed worry over the idea of going back home to face her mother with news about her suspension. He decided to move in with her since he was staying alone in his one-roomed house. By the time they went back to school to write their final exams, Kamagoba's belly had swollen by some inches.

The school administration announced Kayibanda and Kamagoba's expulsion on the radio to inform their parents of the incident. Both their parents and guardians received the news with shock. Kayibanda's guardian wasn't surprised. When his radio blared out the announcement, he was quite stoical. He had witnessed Kayibanda's lecherous ways himself when he nabbed him behind the fence of the paddock massaging a girl's boobs. That incident alone was symptomatic of the impending doom for the son of Kagurutsi. He only hoped Kagurutsi had listened to the announcements.

Kamagoba was an orphan. Her father had committed suicide by hanging himself because of too many debts. He was an insolvent wretch who borrowed to drink rather than pay fees for his children or care for his five wives. Kamagoba was being taken care of by her shrew of a mother. This shrew was going to bed, one night, when she heard on the radio that her daughter had been expelled the previous day. She wondered why Kamagoba had not reached home yet but vowed not to stress herself searching for her daughter. She was tired.

Kamagoba's father had been a fraudster, too. One day he was at a bar with friends and he ordered for them alcohol although he had no money. When he was asked to pay, he agreed with the bar owner that the latter would find him home in the morning and pick up a goat to cover the debt. He had no goat at home, not even chicken. His wife laboured tilling the land and then sold the crops to educate the children.

Bagarukayo walked into Kirinju's compound at dawn when they were still asleep. He knocked on the door and waited. When Kirinju heard the knock, he ordered his wife not to tell anyone that he was in the house.

"Good morning, Madam," Bagarukayo said when Kirinju's wife opened the door. "I have come to collect the goat your husband told me to pick up this morning. He owes me some money."

"Good morning. Sorry, he didn't sleep here," she responded. "I don't know where he slept because he was here in the evening and didn't tell us whether he would come back or not."

Bagarukayo realized that she was lying. He had noticed Kirinju's gumboots that he had worn the previous night.

"I am not leaving this place until your stupid man comes

to give me my goat or pay my money," Bagarukayo asserted while forcing his way into the house. He picked up a rope and threatened to hang himself in the house.

Meanwhile, Kirinju had escaped through the bedroom window. When his wife went to tell him about what was happening and the impending disaster, she was shocked to find an open window and empty bed.

When the news of Bagarukayo's demonstration at Kirinju's home reached the ears of everyone in the village, all those to whom he owed money came and joined the protest. It was agreed by the village chief, in the absence of Kirinju because he had disappeared, that part of his land be sold to pay the debts. When Kirinju learnt about it, he got a rope from a tethered goat in the neighbourhood and hanged himself on a tree. His body was discovered after three days and taken for burial.

Kagurutsi was not at peace now after the radio announcement. He worried about his son. He travelled immediately through the night to Biguri village to meet Chief Bamwine with the intention of seeing to Kayibanda's welfare. He sat with Bamwine on the porch and they talked for over ten hours. It was the crow of a cock that reminded them that they needed to sleep.

Kagurutsi had listened intently and shed tears. His son's past behaviour had been exhumed and he had graduated into a Mafioso of sorts. Bamwine had told Kagurutsi that his son Kayibanda had disappeared with the lady with whom he had been chased from school. He supposed that they were staying together but efforts to trace their whereabouts had proved futile. He had been told that Kayibanda was now a renowned seller of cows in different markets and he had vainly tried several times to find him. Kagurutsi did not know what to do next to trace his son. Miserably, he started his journey to Mpara town the following day to catch a bus back to his home. Throughout the journey, he thought about his son: he was sure that he would visit them in the village one day.

During the long vacation, Kayibanda was recruited into the government's crime prevention brigade and his area of jurisdiction was the whole of Biguri and the neighbouring communities. He was given a gun and the power to recruit other energetic youth that would work with him to combat crime in Biguri.

For the very first time in many years, Kayibanda felt remorseful about deserting Chief Bamwine, who had welcomed him in his home and taken him to school. He decided to go there one evening and apologise for having behaved like a rascal and, at the same time, share with him the good news of finishing school and being recruited to fight crime and cattle rustlers in the Biguri community. He reached Chief Bamwine's home when the latter had just arrived from an electoral campaign - he was vying to represent Biguri in parliament. Bamwine was happy for Kayibanda, but, at the same time, wondered whether he would support him during the campaign against the candidate of the ruling party. Bamwine was a candidate for an opposition political party and it would be difficult for Kayibanda, working for the government, to support an opposition candidate instead of one for the ruling party. The district governor had directed all the crime preventers to comb the villages and campaign for the ruling party candidates and beat up all the opponents' supporters. Kayibanda was now stuck. He was in charge of the area where his onetime guardian was contesting against the ruling party candidate. He very much wanted to support him but the order from the governor barred him, and yet he very much wanted the job. Kayibanda commanded his brigade of crime preventers and launched a campaign against his guardian and in favour of a complete stranger. Bamwine was very furious at Kayibanda's decision and wondered at his actions aimed at suppressing someone who had welcomed him and turned him into what he was now.

Bamwine, because of his great influence as a chief, won the elections despite all the state-inspired violence and intimidation. Kayibanda, together with his goons, went to Bamwine's kraal that night and stole over three hundred head of cattle. They loaded them onto trucks and drove off to the capital. The governor paid Kayibanda handsomely for the great job he had done. He stowed his share of the money into his jacket and disappeared into the darkness.

Kayibanda decided to take a holiday so as to visit his family in Malanga village together with Kamagoba, who was now heavily pregnant. They were to travel in the morning. The road had been tarmacked and he predicted that they'd arrive early enough.

Bekunda was in the kitchen when she heard unusual voices in the compound. She came running, merry, surprised that Kayibanda had come back home after another year of not visiting and the recent worry and tension caused by uncertainty about his whereabouts. What made her happier was that this time he had not come alone; he had come with a wife. She jumped up and ululated. This attracted the neighbours, who rushed into the compound. Kanyeigabo and

Kagurutsi were also home, and they came running and joined Bekunda, circled Kayibanda and Kamagoba and welcomed them in style with hugs and serious pinching of the cheeks to show love and happiness. Even the dog capered around and howled incessantly as other members of the family joined after a long time. The cat meowed in happiness and coiled its tail as it walked away to find its bowl of milk. Soon after the hubbub of excitement had died down, Kamagoba was led inside the house, then into the kitchen. Since it's a custom that women are not visitors, she joined the team that had come together to prepare dinner for the family despite her heavy pregnancy.

The sky in the west was beginning to turn mauve from the impending twilight. Kamagoba poured water from the jerrican into a clay pot and placed it on the tripod of stones around the fire. Others looked on in amazement as they did not expect her to know anything concerning the kitchen and cooking on stones. Then she fanned the fire aflame with her breath and sat back coughing heavily. Thick smoke billowed from the fireplace. Kamagoba was now waiting for the water to boil before she could add millet flour to it to make *karo.*

Bekunda was happy that she had gotten a daughter-in-law. She taught her how to make *emikaro* and *karo* in small baskets known as *endiiro* and advised her to frequently cook it for her husband, Kayibanda. Bekunda was happy that his son had married a woman educated to his level. She was finally relieved that Kayibanda would not come back to marry the dumb Kembaga. She was, however, wrong. Kayibanda was more strongly attached to Kembaga than Kamagoba. During his time in school, he and Kembaga had been exchanging letters and he had promised to marry her. In the letters, however, Kayibanda had said nothing about Kamagoba.

"Kayibanda, thank you for not embarrassing me. Thank you for choosing a beautiful, educated and outstanding woman for marriage. Thank you for making us proud - through choosing beauty with brains," Bekunda said. Her voice was husky and strained. She sat huddled with her son under the mango tree.

Kayibanda's heart was not at peace. His body was there but his soul was at Kembaga's home. He excused himself, pretending to be going to check on the animals in the kraal. However, he disappeared into the darkness and, in a few minutes, he was lurking around Kembaga's home.

Kembaga had seen Kayibanda and the pregnant young woman pass while going home. She knew that Kayibanda would definitely appear anytime, so she had been vigilant. She looked hither and thither expecting a whistle from him, as a sign that she should run to meet his beloved man. She was furious and bitter about the woman she had seen him with, though she wasn't sure about the relationship between them. She sat in the compound with a swollen heart and cheeks like she had cud in them. Jealousy was torturing her and she was about to burst. Finally, she heard a whistle and ran to meet her man.

He noticed that she wasn't happy as she got close to him. The moon was young and had just appeared and shone dimly in the east. He opened out his arms for her and soon she was nestled against his chest, sobbing.

"You lied that you would come and marry me. I have seen your pregnant wife. Why did you lie to me, Kayibanda?" Kembaga complained.

"Honeycomb, I am very sorry but I love you and I will marry you. This woman I have come back with, I am stuck with her. When she goes back to her home, I will write to you to join me in Mpara town. I am eternally yours, dear. She made me fall into her coquettish trap. I was tempted to kiss her lips while in the library at school. The result was that we were dismissed and she had nowhere to go. So we ended up living together," Kayibanda confessed, his voice filled with humbleness and love.

They sat down, and she lay her head on his lap. The night was silent, save for the frogs that sang ebulliently in turns in the nearby ditch that had been filled with stagnant water. They kissed each other and both got electrified. They made quick love right there on the carpet of grass and bade each other goodbye.

Kembaga had finished her primary leaving examinations and was now waiting for Kayibanda to marry her. She didn't want to continue with her studies despite the fact that she was from a well-off family and her mother still could afford to sell some cows and pay her school fees up to whatever level she desired. She was not willing to continue because, in every class, she would bring up the rear at the end of every term. All she wanted now was to get married and the only man she wanted was Kayibanda. She was determined to fight for his love until he chased away the 'bitch'.

Kayibanda, on the other hand, was torn between the two

young women. He didn't know what to do. He loved Kembaga deeply but Kamagoba was heavily pregnant and educated. Bekunda, his mother, was happy that Kayibanda had finally decided to marry a lady other than Kembaga. Kagurutsi was happy, too, that he had got involved with an educated woman and they were expecting a child. Bekunda wouldn't forgive him if he married Kembaga!

"Should I marry two wives?" Kayibanda mused. "Let me think about it. But I need more money to buy land and cattle." Kayibanda thought the whole night without arriving at a solution.

While Kayibanda and his father were huddled in tête-à-tête in the compound, an announcement was aired on radio that the results for Senior Six final examinations had been released. Kayibanda's name and that of Kamagoba were read among those who had gotten government scholarships abroad and were required to get in touch with the Minister of Education immediately for clearance and to pick up acceptance forms from the university. They both received the news with great happiness. Kayibanda decided quickly that they should travel back to Mpara town on the Sunday night.

Part Three

Kayibanda left the country with Kamagoba and their four-month-old baby boy. They had both been given scholarships to study at Tara University in a neighbouring country. They travelled by bus for twenty hours to reach the university. Kayibanda was to study economics while Kamagoba was given law.

During the first semester at the university, Kayibanda was very bright and read widely. He would challenge everyone, including the lecturers, because of his hypothetical questioning. He became a darling of many and would often be invited to talk to high school leavers and encourage them to study further. One day, Kayibanda was invited to an economic forum as the guest of honour. As the seminar peacefully progressed, his laptop battery went flat because he had been using it for typing his speech. He pulled out a charger from the bag, excused himself, walked towards the wall, plugged the charger into the socket and put the pin into the laptop, which started charging. When time for lunch came, he didn't like the food they had prepared. It was junk, so he moved to the nearby upscale restaurant and had a local buffet for lunch. As he drank beer to wash down the lunch, he remembered that he had forgotten his laptop in an open place and it was susceptible to being stolen since he was the only one with a laptop. He had stolen it from a tourist in Mpanga town and learnt only to use Microsoft Word to type his things. When he returned to the premises from lunch, he found that his valuable item had been stolen! It was nowhere to be seen; there was only the charger plugged into the socket with the wire hanging out.

Kayibanda asked a few youth who had been around. They told him that none of them had seen anyone unplugging the laptop from the charger. The youth he had been invited to train had now stolen his computer and left the charger in the socket. He reached his seat, ensconced himself on a chair facing the audience and forgot about the laptop.

When it was time for him to address the youth – to motivate them, to encourage and mentor them – Kayibanda was handed the microphone by the master of ceremonies. However, the laptop on which he had been typing his notes had been stolen, so he had nothing to talk about. He quickly hatched a plan to take care of this. The ululations from the youth made him happy but none of them knew what he had planned to speak to them about.

He started by introducing himself as a veteran witchdoctor who had invaluable experience in catching thieves, blinding and crippling them, and killing them whenever necessary. The audience sharply looked at him, bewildered as though they had seen Satan about to devour them. Even his fellow speakers scanned him carefully to know whether he was really fine. They asked themselves what he had eaten when he had gone out to lunch - perhaps wasps, one suggested!

Kayibanda continued with the speech amidst the confusion that registered on the faces of the audience. He added that whoever had ever lost anything should stand up and come forward, that the thief will bring back the stolen property right there crawling like a sn..... Before he could finish uttering the word "snake," a boy of about seventeen got up quickly from his seat as though he had seen a snake crawling between his legs. With indescribable rapidity, he got out and came back after three minutes, laptop in hand. He was panting. He walked briskly to the platform, threw the laptop down on the table, rushed out again and disappeared through the slightly open gate.

Everyone was confused as Kayibanda picked up the laptop from where the boy had thrown it. No one knew what was going on except Kayibanda himself. He laughed his lungs out and told everyone succinctly that it was a trick he played to get back his stolen computer. Everyone laughed and praised Kayibanda for possessing incomparable wisdom. They all admired his trick of getting a confident thief to give up what he has stolen through unenforceable threats. The MC asked the audience to calm down and soon Kayibanda switched on the laptop and resumed his speech. The thief had hidden the laptop in the orchard near the hall where the seminar was taking place.

Two years into the course, Kayibanda's performance deteriorated. It was marked mainly by failures, and Kayibanda was threatened with discontinuation by the university because of the very many retakes he had to do. This dismal performance was due to Kayibanda spending more time boasting and drinking than actually studying.

Kayibanda had now come to hate the economics course. He changed to law. However, after one semester in Law School, he gave up and decided to return to his home country and ask for a job in the military government. He had hated his shrewish wife; all his thoughts were with Kembaga.

Kayibanda plotted for Kamagoba's death. He planned it in such a manner that he would not be suspected of killing her. Kayibanda agreed with Kamagoba that he should return to Kalenga with their son since he could now walk on his own and was making it difficult for her to concentrate on her studies. Kayibanda was to leave the toddler in his friend's custody in Mpanga, the capital city of Kalenga, and return to meet Kamagoba at the beach on the fourteenth of December. On the tenth of December Kayibanda left Kalenga through the southern border for Hada beach in Tanya country. He reached early to reconnoitre the way and plan how to accomplish his mission. On the thirteenth, indeed, Kamagoba showed up and they went swimming together at dusk. Kayibanda took her to the deep part of the beach and drowned her. He tied her to a stone and it sank to the abyss of the sea with her. He executed the mission very efficiently and sneaked out of the water, taking another route that he had reconnoitered the day before, changed clothes and disappeared into the darkness.

The following morning, Kayibanda was in the slums of Mpanga resting at his friend's place, stuck with his son whom he had named Rwehakanuzire. Kayibanda now needed money to sustain himself and his son until he was able to get a job. He wrote to Kembaga, informing her that she should prepare to come to the city in the next few months. He needed her to join him and take care of Rwehakanuzire, as he was busy looking for a job. With the little money that he had, Kayibanda rented a *muzigo* in one of the suburbs. It was among four one-room *mizigo* in a row, each having a door but no window. There was no ceiling, too; so while resting in his *muzigo,* he would hear other occupants' conversations, and, in the middle of the night, their sounds of love-making. The voices would make him sick to the marrow.

Kayibanda would sometimes take care of the baby during the day and move around at night, robbing people together with his new-found criminal gang. He had started regretting abandoning his course at the university and choosing to suffer under a military government with an idiot as president. He and his gang would stage ambushes, robbing people of hard cash and killing them.

That is how Kayibanda got by before he got a job. Soon, they started getting daylight deals, but it was getting difficult to do them because of the child. One day, Kayibanda woke up early in the morning and left the child with the neighbour. He travelled to the village with the intention of picking up Kembaga and bringing her to the city. He arrived at Kembaga's place when darkness was about to settle in. He whistled to alert Kembaga to his presence. She was in the kitchen cooking and heard the whistle at the third attempt. She happily jumped out of the kitchen and marched towards where the sound of the whistle had emanated from. She was very dirty and hadn't had a bath since morning. So when Kayibanda seized her hand, it was sticky with sweat.

"Come on, let's go. I have come for you and we are going right now," Kayibanda said impatiently while pulling her in the direction of the road.

"I am dirty and wearing tattered clothes. Let me shower first and put on my new clothes. We can then leave, my dear," Kembaga pleaded.

"No, I have no time. If you are coming, come. If you don't want, please go and forget about me. I have carried for you new clothes and shoes. Let's go. You will bathe at the river and we shall board the night bus. I have not been to our home and I do not want anyone to see me," Kayibanda said, sounding serious.

They both disappeared into the darkness and reached the river. She bathed and put on the clothes he had bought for her.

On his way to Kembaga's place, he had known he would find her unready. So he had passed by the market where he had cursorily rummaged through a heap of *mivumba* and picked a yellow dress with a long slit. He had also gone to a shop, too, and ordered size forty-three shoes. He knew Kembaga had large, long and fat feet.

"Wow, you look stunning," Kayibanda said after she had drawn on the shoes. The dress had a middle slit long enough to expose her smooth thighs.

"The only thing you forgot to buy was a pair of knickers or bermudas," she complained as they walked out of the river to the bank.

By sunrise the following day, they were in the *muzigo*, already breakfasting on chapatti and samosa. Rwehakanuzire was already beginning to get acclimated to his new mother. Kembaga had asked about Kamagoba and Kayibanda had lied that he had ordered her to return to their home and had remained with the baby. Kembaga had believed without any reservations.

One day, Kayibanda was arrested with his gang by the police when they attempted to break into the local bank. The magistrate's court sentenced him and two other members of the gang to prison. Six of them had been arrested but, to his surprise, only three were tried and sentenced. He was worried only about his wife Kembaga and the child now. He had left her with money for only three meals and he had expected to return home with bulging pockets, but now his expectations had been scuttled. The other three members of the gang had been army officers and were released on bail and demoted.

Kembaga was worried when three days elapsed without her seeing her husband. She didn't know what to do now. Kayibanda had paid rent for six months, and there were still four months to go. She needed not worry about rent; she only had to worry about food and other needs. She heard over the radio that Kayibanda and his gang of robbers had been imprisoned and she wept. She now needed to survive by any means possible until he returned from prison.

Kembaga started moving around to look for what to do. She was not educated enough to get a government job somewhere.

She only qualified to wash other people's laundry or to wait at the restaurant or clean offices. The only barricade was a child now – Rwehakanuzire the son of Kayibanda. She settled for a waiting job where she would work only eight hours a day every day except Sundays, when she would take leave. She was to be paid on a daily basis. She reached an agreement with one of her neighbours to keep her son for eight hours each day at an agreed amount of money.

Kembaga started working as a waiter at a certain restaurant in town. She was happy, though worried about her husband who had been imprisoned. When Kembaga told Martha about her ordeal, she laughed at her and advised her to forget about the husband. Martha was a friend Kembaga had met at the restaurant. When they found out that they spoke the same language, they became quite tight. She argued that, with the government in power and the existing level of impunity, her husband would rot in prison. Kembaga thought about it for a few days and decided there was need for her to always look nice in case any prospective suitor came along since she was now working at a public place.

Martha had been working at the restaurant for the past two years and she knew all the corners of the city. She would work for eight hours during the day and rush back home to rest. Then, at eleven in the night, she would wake up and go on the streets to vend sex. This would go on up to five in the morning. That was when she would return to her home, refresh and go to her other work. Kembaga was soon cajoled into taking up the sex trade as a means of earning extra income. Though she was reluctant at first when Martha had sold her the idea, she soon warmed up to the prospect of joining the trade.

One day, Kayibanda was summoned from his lice-and bedbug-infested prison cell by a warder to see his visitors. The warder opened the cell and instructed Kayibanda to follow him. The prisoner wondered who the visitors were. He had spent months in the cells without experiencing life outside with its fresh air and sunlight. His cell had only one door without any window or ventilator. The yellow bulb on the ceiling burnt incessantly, day in and day out, and provided light and warmth to the room. He was surprised to see three men from his gang who had not been incarcerated with them six months earlier. They had come to pick him up together with two others with whom he had been incarcerated.

"The president is looking for professional assassins to help him silence his enemies. If you are ready to take it, you are going to be freed. If not, you will die in prison," Muteguya said and sniggered. "You will receive guns, machetes, vehicles and everything needed to carry out the job," Muteguya added and pulled at his cigarette.

Kayibanda examined his fellow inmates to see whether they were in agreement or not. Kayibanda was worried about the wellbeing of his family, so he accepted without asking any questions. The other two guys, however, feared the deal and refused. Muteguya cocked his gun and shot them in full view of the prison wardens.

Kayibanda got scared at what he had seen. He was bundled into the army pick-up which proceeded to disappear into the cloud of dust through the open gate.

Kayibanda was taken to State House to meet the president. He was a tall, dark man who spoke broken English in a deep voice.

Muteguya, Kayibanda and two others signed an agreement to be discreet and report directly to the president immediately after the successful mission.

The president gave both men a bundle of money each and dismissed them with an order to report the following day for a mission. The president, Ongoi, had been in power for two years now and was facing stiff opposition from churches and the elite. He had overthrown a civilian president, Okot, who had been away in Singapore attending a Commonwealth meeting of heads of state. The civilian president, whose designation had once been executive prime minister, had, himself, overthrown the colonial constitution which had a non-executive president who doubled as a king of one of the communities in the country. Okot forced the king into exile in the United Kingdom and assumed the office of president with executive powers. Ongoi now, after assuming the presidency, suspended the constitution and parliament and ruled by decree.

Kayibanda walked away, not believing that he had become the president's hatchet man. Now that he had a bundle of money in his pocket, he started thinking out a plan of getting a nice house. He pinched himself to make sure that he was awake; he thought it was all a dream. He passed by a city suburb and paid one year's rent for a three-bedroom house and hired a truck. He sat at the front in the co-driver's seat, and off they went to collect his family and other belongings.

Kembaga had been resting on the bed when he felt a zephyr of breath on her cheek. Kayibanda had kissed her and woken her up. She couldn't believe what her eyes saw. She had come back from work a while ago and had been resting so she could wake up at ten and prepare for the streets. She felt her heart leap with joy upon seeing Kayibanda suddenly after the six months he had spent in prison.

"Get up! We shall pack up our belongings and leave at once. I have found a good house where we shall be staying," Kayibanda said with authority.

Without questioning her husband's sudden decision, Kembaga packed all the clothes in a bag and all the utensils in boxes. Their room had very few things. They could only half-fill a pick-up. However, the huge amount of money Kayibanda had received from the president blinded him to this reality and he hired a Fuso truck. In a mere two hours they were already in the new house, located near the city.

Kembaga was surprised at the sudden appearance of her husband. She was even more surprised at the sudden change from a ramshackle to a furnished house now. When they had finished arranging the house together, she thought they would sit down and talk. To her chagrin, however, she heard her husband making an urgent appointment with someone by radio call.

Muteguya and his gang of assassins sat over dinner, al fresco, behind the hotel building where the waitress had organised for them. They wrote down a requisition they would hand over to the president the following day. In the requisition were twelve guns with ammunition, two Land Rover vehicles with free fuel access and maintenance, swords and grenades. After they had finished writing the requisition, they each drank four beers and asked the busboy to get them prostitutes. The following morning, they met the president at State House with their requisition and he authorised his comptroller to provide whatever they required. They drove out with an order to finish off a certain stubborn minister. In one hour they had completed the mission and given a report to the president.

After six years of working for the president as a special assassin, Kayibanda decided to take leave and check on his people in Malanga village. The president himself granted Kayibanda permission and even gave him a lot of money to spend while away. He drove to the village in the army combat fatigues and in an army vehicle with his wife Kembaga and children. He went with the intention to cajole his father Kagurutsi to take him to the headquarters of Bachwezi so that he could receive the powers to change into anything in case of an attack. This would enable him to execute his duties well since he was now mature. Kagurutsi was surprised to see an army vehicle park in the compound of his home, more surprised to see his son alight, and most surprised to see Kembaga also alight with three children! Kagurutsi now looked very miserable. Bekunda was sick in the house and Kanyeigabo had run away to the city to look for a job. The cows had since died of a strange disease that attacked the village and Kagurutsi had planned to go back to Biguri the coming month. The whole home was disorganised.

The following day, the family was in the car heading to Biguri village again to settle there, more than forty-five years since Kagurutsi had fled the place because of drought. The few cows that had been in the custody of Chief Bamwine had been used to educate Kayibanda and the remaining ones had been stolen at the behest of the same Kayibanda. The chief was furious when he saw Kayibanda, especially in the army attire and the vehicle.

Parliament had been dismissed and so Bamwine was living a quiet life in the village looking after his few animals. He had sent all his children abroad to study there when the military government was ushered in for fear of their lives. Now, Kayibanda, whom he had mentored and educated, but who had later tormented him with guns and violence, was back. Moreover, in full combat fatigues with his father, mother, wife and children.

Kayibanda did not know that when his goons stole Bamwine's cows, his father's were also among them. The close friendship that Bamwine and Kagurutsi had enjoyed for decades had been strained by Kayibanda. Kagurutsi learnt with utter shock that he had come to Biguri village with empty hands and that he would live like a peasant because of his son's malfeasance. He had left the village many years ago a rich man with a big herd of cattle and now he had nothing! Bamwine forgave Kayibanda even when he had not asked for forgiveness. He welcomed them into his home again. The following day he went with them to trace the boundaries of the land again.

Kagurutsi had land which had been amalgamated with Bamwine's many years ago. Now that he was back, that land had to be separated. Chunks of land with a small hut on it, with him now living like a peasant who had never had anything like cattle.

When they had come back from the Bachwezi, Kayibanda bought twenty head of cattle for his father and off he drove with his family back to the city. Kagurutsi started life again with twenty cows and three sheep. He started building a bigger hut. When it was completed, he thatched it with grass and stayed there with his wife Bekunda.

Kayibanda was now equipped with Bachwezi powers and vowed to test them when he reached the city. He now saw no use for the gun since he could change into a lion and eat up whoever he was assigned to kill. He smiled to himself whenever he thought of the automatic power that possessed him when attacked. As he was still silently wallowing in his power, the president communicated by radio call and summoned him to State House in fifteen hours. The following morning, he reported to State House and the president informed him, by word of mouth, that he was now the leader of the assassins and that he should look for the people to work with. Kayibanda wondered what happened to Muteguya and others in his absence.

"Recruit two people who will be under you and report here tomorrow morning," the president said angrily and slammed the door to his private room behind him, leaving Kayibanda alone in the boardroom with his mouth open. The following day Kayibanda reported with his fellows and was ordered to assassinate the Chief Justice.

Muteguya and his gang had been given an order to assassinate the Inspector General of Police but they passed by the bar and drank themselves silly. When the time came to shoot, they failed in their mission and their target ran away. The following day, the man was heard on international news channels talking of how he escaped being assassinated by the president's assassins. He had run out of the country in the night and managed to call a press conference. When Muteguya went to report the incident, the president shattered their jaws with bullets sprayed into their mouths.

The following day Kayibanda reported to the president after he had executed the job with his new gang. The president thanked them but demanded evidence that the Chief Justice had been killed. While he was making himself comfortable in the chair, television brought breaking news that the Chief Justice's car had caught fire and burst into flames, killing the Chief Justice and his driver. The president was happy and opened a safe and handed them huge sums of money.

When he was driving home, Kayibanda started reminiscing about the number of innocent people who had died at his hands under the orders of the president. They were very many. He had made a lot of money and it was now time he fled the country. He knew that sooner or later he would fall victim to the ruthless dictator. He hatched a plan. His wife and two children needed travel documents. He himself had one.

The following morning, he took his wife and children to the immigration office to process their passports. He had established a lot of connections now and he started securing a place for his family outside the country. He finally, through a friend, got a country in Europe where he took his family. He returned to his home country, wishing to work for one or two more years before running away.

When Kayibanda came back, one of his friends whispered to him that he would be killed and that he himself was on the run. The president was no longer giving him orders to kill. However, there were many assassinations and he was wondering who the new assassins were. His fellows had maligned him to the president while he was away. They had alleged that Kayibanda was working with Okot's spies on a scheme to assassinate the president. The president had believed the rumour and ordered Kayibanda's shooting the moment he returned. Kayibanda tried to reach the president by radio in vain. He knew now that he was finished. He had spent all the money on him to cater for the family in Europe and thought he would come back and make more. He was stuck.

Okot, the ousted president, still had loyal soldiers in Ongoi's military government. Sometimes they would kill many people and create a state of insecurity and Ongoi's government would receive heavy criticism from the international community. There were very many killings, including of high-profile people, and the president would wonder who was killing them. He had received intelligence that Okot was hiding in Tanya and an attack on Kalenga to oust him was imminent. Meanwhile Kayibanda had sneaked out through the southern border to Tanya and had met with Okot's rebels planning to attack Ongoi's illegal government.

When Ongoi learnt through intelligence about the rolling disaster from Tanya, he ordered a battalion of soldiers to attack Tanya in the south of Kalenga. The soldiers killed many rebels who had been preparing to launch the first attack.

Okot sought military assistance from the Tanyan president and launched an attack on Kalenga on December seventeenth. By January the rebels had entered the capital city and Ongoi had fled into exile with his family and children. Kayibanda had played an important role in Ongoi's ousting, and when Okot assumed the presidency Kayibanda was rewarded with the defence portfolio.

Okot ruled for only one year during which he organised the country and restored security. He called for elections, a new constitution and the reinstatement of parliament. This was welcomed with excitement and all those who had fled the country came back to participate in the elections.

Elections were held and only three political parties took part. According to the constitution, the political party which won the most seats in Parliament formed a government, and its chairman became the president of the country. Okot's party, Kalenga People's Congress, was the most popular one, followed by the Democratic Party and the newly formed Kalenga People's Movement, whose chairman was Kayibanda.

Kayibanda resigned his position as Minister of Defence and went to contest in Biguri as a member of parliament on the ticket of his new political party that had only a handful of supporters. He was rejected on the grounds that he was a former criminal from Ongoi's government and also not a citizen of Kalenga. His rival for the seat won with ninety per cent of the vote and the invalid votes were more than those Kayibanda had got.

Kalenga People's Congress won the elections with seventy per cent of the seats in parliament and the Democratic Party came second with thirty per cent. Kalenga's People's Movement of Kayibanda didn't win any seat in parliament. Okot assumed the presidency of the country. On May twelfth, Okot opened parliament with a new constitution and he was sworn in by the Chief Justice as the president. After three days, he appointed his cabinet ministers, junior ministers, permanent secretaries, Inspector of Police, commander of the army and vice president. Kayibanda had been full of expectation that he would appear on the list of ministers or be appointed army commander but, to his chagrin, he wasn't anywhere on any list.

Kayibanda wasn't the only one who felt let down. His close friends and comrades were angry that Okot had not appointed them. Kayibanda met with forty of them to look for a way to survive in Okot's government as rejects. He chaired the meeting and Runkunku took the minutes. Kayibanda came up with a plot to oust the government, but what reasons would they give for rebelling against the elected government? When they finished the meeting, the majority of the participants had chosen the idea of a war against the Okot's government. Thirty-nine of them had voted to popularise their cause basing on these points:

- ☐ Corruption
- ☐ Biting poverty
- ☐ Insecurity
- ☐ Tribalism
- ☐ Vote rigging and commercialisation of politics
- ☐ Excessive presidential powers
- ☐ Cronyism
- ☐ Land grabbing
- ☐ Twenty-five per cent unemployment

Kayibanda was elected the leader. They agreed on the date to launch the campaign against the government, which was ninth July, at Freedom Square. Each of the forty men who had attended the meeting was tasked with mobilising at least twenty others and coming with them to Freedom Square on the agreed date. Kayibanda contacted local and international media houses and alerted them to the date of the campaign launch.

Mpanga city was paralysed on ninth July, when different security agents used teargas and live bullets to disperse the peaceful demonstrators that had occupied Freedom Square to air their grievances against the government in the presence of cameras. A dozen people were killed and scores arrested and imprisoned.

The following day, Kayibanda held a press conference and warned the government that he would go to the bush and fight against it if the listed problems were not tackled urgently. The president ordered for Kayibanda's arrest and appointed a group of people to muckrake him and expose the crimes he had committed under President Ongoi.

When Kayibanda heard about his planned arrest and the muckraking order, he knew he was in trouble. He sat down with his group and briefed them about the guns he had acquired. They decided to launch a bush war against the Okot government. They broke into a bank and took off with all the money they could lay their hands on. They had killed seven bank guards. They also took off with the guards' guns.

When the soldiers who were not loyal to Okot learnt that a new rebel movement had been formed, they decided to escape with their guns and join the rebels in the bush. By end of the year, the rebels had increased in number from forty to three hundred. They vowed to make Kalenga difficult for Okot to govern. Their first assault against the government was an attack on a barracks, which they looted clean. They left many loyal soldiers dead and scores injured. They acquired guns, grenades and military outfits. Okot vowed to crush the 'swine' that had started undermining the peace of the people. He directed his army commander to launch a war against the rebels and arrest them all or kill them and bring him the head of their ring leader, Kayibanda the barbarian. Opio, the army commander, organised four hundred soldiers to surround and attack the rebels. He dispatched them in the night and they spent the day moving towards the rebel camp north of Mpanga city. The following day, Opio flew to the battlefield in a chopper. When he had arrived and given orders by radio call for the ground soldiers to attack the rebels, he boarded the chopper again to return to army headquarters. A missile hit his helicopter, which burst into flames and spiraled back to the ground. The rebels now descended on the soldiers and massacred them like cows.

News of the incident caught the world's attention. The government had lost hundreds of soldiers as well as the army commander. It was a huge embarrassment for Okot and a huge boost to the rebels' morale. Very many people now started joining the rebels in the bush for training; these included intellectuals fresh from university. Some members of Okot's army also joined the rebels. Kayibanda now had over two thousand rebels at his disposal while the government army had a strength of one thousand five hundred.

International pressure mounted on Okot to negotiate with the rebels but he insisted that he would crush and eat them like samosas.

At the nascent stage of the rebellion, Kayibanda's rebels survived entirely on cassava and beans stolen from the neighbouring villages. However, when they increased in number they started eating posho without any sauce. They would use the money stolen from the bank to buy food and medicine. Or sometimes they would attack hospitals and steal medicine and other items like mattresses and blankets. Kayibanda was in and out of the bush because he always had meetings to attend in different foreign countries.

One day, he was motoring south in his open jeep when he found the road had been closed with spiked planks of timber. Four soldiers stood at the roadside holding rifles while others sat in the shade of a tree playing cards. When he suddenly saw the roadblock he braked sharply and the tyres screeched on the tarmac. The government soldiers all got up hurriedly and seized their rifles, readying themselves to attack the enemy. Two of the soldiers strolled over to the car with their guns cocked. To the surprise of the soldiers, they found that no one was in the vehicle much as the engine was running and the gear lever was in neutral, the handbrake on. Kayibanda had changed into a snake and hidden under the driver's seat. The soldiers thought that the driver and the occupants had jumped out, but again asked themselves how the driver could have managed to find time to park the vehicle properly without driving over the planks. They called out to their comrades to come and see the miracle that had happened. In the process, the snake crept out of the car into the bush. When the soldiers had all gathered around the vehicle, Kayibanda flung a grenade at the jeep. The jeep burst into flames and killed all.

The snake hissed and peeped to see whether there was any survivor. However, all the soldiers were burning like wood. The snake changed back into its human form and drove off in the army Land Rover that the soldiers had used. Kayibanda laughed uncontrollably as he drove and almost had a head on collision with an oncoming trailer truck. He skidded off to the right side and managed to stop in the nearby bushes. The driver of the truck got scared and jumped out, leaving the vehicle to move alone. He died instantly on coming into contact with the ground. The truck crashed into the burning jeep and also caught fire.

Kayibanda tried to reverse back onto the road in vain. The Land Rover produced an awkward noise and emitted wreaths of smoke through the exhaust pipe. When he opened the bonnet to see what was wrong, he noticed that the radiator had cracked. He had damaged it when he hit a big stone.

Kayibanda abandoned the Land Rover in the bushes and moved back into the road to find other means to travel to the city centre. He had undressed the driver and put on his clothes. He was now a civilian and no one would think of him as a rebel.

Kayibanda walked through the village paths, avoiding the main road. By 9 pm, he was already in the city centre, where he boarded a taxi to meet his informers in the suburbs. He was wearing a bowler hat, and had a lush moustache and beard to erase all suspicion about his true identity.

Kayibanda's rebels sneaked into the city the following day and robbed several banks. They took off with huge sums of money after killing many of the guards on duty.

Okot was furious at Kayibanda's actions against his legitimate government. His army had failed totally to track the rebels because every time they planned an attack, they would find the rebels more than ready to defend themselves. Sometimes, they would only see darkness when they reached the rebel camps and end up falling in their traps instead. Okot was about to capitulate because Kyibanda had made his government ungovernable. However, he was advised by those who knew Kayibanda better that a Muchweezi like Kayibanda needed to be counter-fought with the same ideology.

****

Meanwhile, in Europe where Kembaga lived with her children, they were taken good care of by Kayibanda's associates. From feeding to rent to school fees for the children. Sometimes Kayibanda would spend seven months without checking on his family.

Kembaga, being a young woman, felt neglected because of Kayibanda's itinerant lifestyle. She longed for someone to act as a substitute in the short run. However, she feared to take this path because her husband would frequently turn up unannounced and she didn't want to be caught out.

One day, Kayibanda sent her money through Gatete. He reached the apartment block where Kayibanda's family stayed. As soon as his car pulled into the parking yard, he saw Kembaga closing the entrance door to their apartment behind her.

Kembaga had been going out to meet a man who had been insistent. She had rung him and told him that she was coming that evening to spend time with him at his apartment. She wore high-heeled shoes and a skimpy dress with a wide open neck that exposed her cleavage and bra straps to full advantage. Gatete was also struck by her stunning beauty. He had always met her in the dark or in candlelight every time he delivered a package from Kayibanda. He alighted from the car and moved towards where Kembaga stood, waiting to see who the visitor was.

"Wow you look very beautiful," Gatete said. "I have just realised that you are the most beautiful woman I have ever seen in this world." Then he gathered her into a hug.

"Really? Are you sure about what you are saying, friend of my husband, or you are just joking in coquetry," Kembaga said and smiled into his face.

Gatete was also longing for a woman. When he hugged Kembaga, her full breasts pricked his chest and his body became electrified. His trousers had started bulging between the legs by the time he released her from his arms. The feeling was mutual. When Kembaga noticed what was happening in Gatete's trousers, she suggested that they should get back into the car and go for a drink somewhere.

Gatete spent the night with Kembaga at his apartment. He surely enjoyed Kembaga's company and so did she enjoy his. They decided to meet every weekend at his apartment thereafter.

Kembaga was mad, now that her feelings were fully aroused. She now thought that it was too long to wait for a weekend to come around for another moment of glory. In the middle of the night, she picked up the phone and invited Gatete to come to the apartment. She assured him that the children were all asleep.

Gatete drove very quickly, overtaking carelessly like a drunk driver. Indeed, he was drunk with horniness. In five minutes he was at the door. He was about to knock on the door when he saw the door opening. In a few minutes they were entwined on a couch. They completely forgot to close the door. They only remembered to close it when they were done.

****

Meanwhile another rebel group had been formed and their sole aim was to assassinate high-profile people so that the populace would view Okot's government in the same light as Ongoi's. Okot's government was on its knees and he chose a date to hold a dialogue with the rebels. Kayibanda represented the rebels together with his ten senior commanders. Off they went to Tanya to meet with Okot. The meeting was chaired by the Tanyan president and it ended without bearing fruit. Both parties didn't accept the other's demands and were not ready to cede ground. Kayibanda had demanded that he be appointed army commander and his rebels be integrated into the national army. Okot, on the other hand, had suggested that Kayibanda be appointed State Minister of Transport and Works. They both left the dialogue angry and vowed to crush each other.

Kayibanda, meanwhile, was very promiscuous in the bush. He had impregnated over one hundred and thirty women and all were in the rebel camp being taken care of and protected by *kadogo* soldiers. Some of the women had children already and many others were still pregnant. With the exception of the top commanders, other rebels were not allowed to bring their wives into the camp. As a result, some of the other rebels would sneak and help themselves to Kayibanda's numerous women.

The discriminatory policy about women angered some of the rebels and they plotted against Kayibanda. They sneaked into his tent one night intent on killing him, but, when one had cocked to shoot him, Kayibanda changed into a crocodile and swallowed three of his attackers. Those who ran away told their fellows about what they had witnessed and, from then on, Kayibanda became the most feared commander.

****

Gatete was in real love with Kembaga now. He started feeling jealous whenever he met Kayibanda to receive a package for his family in Europe. Kembaga's love only belonged to Kayibanda, however. What she was doing with Gatete or other men simply arose out of a critical physical need because her husband was always busy.

Gatete didn't know this. He mistook her need for sex all the time as love. One day, he passed by the supermarket and bought flowers and an engagement ring for Kembaga. He was determined to ask for her hand in marriage and was ready to elope with her. But what about the children? he asked himself... Ahhh, he answered himself, we shall put them on a plane to Kalenga so that they can find their father in the bush.

It was already afternoon when he pulled into the parking of the apartment. Kembaga had been in the window combing her hair. When she saw Gatete, she knew that she was dead because Kayibanda had arrived in the night. She tried to signal to him to go back but he didn't see the signals. He marched right to the house with a bouquet of flowers in his left hand and a bottle of wine in the other. He had come determined to sell his idea to Kembaga and he was sure she would not refuse. Kayibanda was in the sitting room having breakfast. When Gatete drew the curtain at the entrance, his eyes sat on Kayibanda at the dining table. He immediately threw the flowers into the flower garden and remained with only the bottle of Four Cousins wine.

"Surprise!" Gatete announced his arrival with a guffaw and marched over to where Kayibanda sat.

"Oh my friend, how did you know that I came? Did you see me at the airport last night? I tried to call you to pick me up but your phone was unavailable," Kayibanda said as he rose from the chair to greet his friend.

"My friend told me that he saw you getting into a cab, so I decided to surprise you this morning with this huge bottle of your favourite wine. You know I care about you, my rebel friend. How is the bush?" Gatete lied. He was himself impressed with how quickly he had composed the lie. He had not known that he was such a competent liar.

"We are moving on well. I promise you that, by next year, I will be the president of Kalenga by hook or crook. Okot must go," Kayibanda said.

Meanwhile in the bedroom, Kembaga knew that she was finished. Her heart was pounding wildly. She believed that Gatete was poor at lying and would be caught out. When she heard their laughter floating in from the sitting room, she breathed a sigh of relief and marched out to serve Gatete breakfast.

When Kayibanda was ready to return to Kalenga, Gatete saw it as an opportunity to carry out his plan. He was feeling terribly jealous of Kayibanda's presence. He escorted Kayibanda up to the airport to make sure that he was really gone. The children were at school and it was a sunny afternoon when Gatete drove from the airport back to Kembaga's apartment.

"My dear, I missed you so much and longed to be with you," Gatete said as he reached for the ring in his pocket. "Here, will you marry me? This is an engagement ring," Gatete added.

Kembaga's eyes almost popped out of the sockets when he knelt down to propose to her. She only wanted exciting sex from him but not marriage.

"Are you crazy Gatete or what? I am a married woman and, interestingly, to your friend. We have four children together and I cannot disappoint him any single day. We are just friends, sexual friends, and nothing more," Kembaga said with a disinterested look at Gatete.

Gatete pleaded with Kembaga in vain. She turned down his request to elope to another country and start a new life together. She emphasised that their relationship was based on sex and sex alone and that he shouldn't demand nor expect anything more than that.

All along they had been in the sitting room standing. Gatete came closer to Kembaga and kissed her on the lips and the cleavage. She kissed him back feverishly. He tore her dress in haste for he didn't have time to look for the zip. He noticed that she did not have knickers or a bra on. He pushed her to the couch and they made love. He lifted her up without separating and walked to the bedroom, where they crowned the afternoon glory.

Gatete walked down the stairs naked and found his clothes in the sitting room. He put them on and drove away, disappointed that she had refused his offer but again happy that they had made ecstatic love.

Afterwards, Gatete spent two months without communicating to Kembaga. He would bring the packages from Kayibanda and drop them at the apartment without saying anything. They soon got used to each other's silence. However, one night, Kembaga couldn't control herself anymore. She reached for her phone and called Gatete to give him the good news of acceptance. Gatete had been driving back home. It had been snowing heavily. Upon receiving the good news, he made a sudden U-turn in the middle of the road and a bus crushed him dead. At the other end the call was still on and Kembaga only heard a screech and a loud bang, then the phone went off. When she called back, the phone was unavailable. It was the following day that she watched the news of the accident on television. The pain she felt went deep, right into the marrow. She thought about all the nice sex Gatete had been giving her, and she reproached herself for causing his death. Had she accepted to elope with him, he wouldn't have died then. Or had she called him during the day or sent him a text message, he would not have died. It was her secret and she vowed to die with it. Meanwhile she realised that she was three months pregnant and her husband had last slept with her two months before. That meant the pregnancy was Gatete's.

Kembaga rushed to see a doctor to get rid of the orphaned foetus. Gatete had infected Kembaga with gonorrhea and she had passed it on to Kayibanda, who took it to his innumerable women in the rebel camp. Soon even his officers got a share of the disease, too. They had to ransack a hospital to acquire drugs for their illness.

When Kayibanda had acquired enough guns and ammunition for all his rebels, numbering two thousand now, he called a meeting with senior rebels one night. They planned the final attack on Okot's selfish and murderous government. They sat through the night and shared ideas, with everyone giving their views on how to execute the plan. Their mission was to carry out a grand attack once and capture power just as they had ousted Ongoi's military government.

Kayibanda spoke last and lectured them according to what his informers had told him. He was satisfied that the seniors would pass on the plan of the attack. He authorised them to pass the minutes of the meeting to their juniors the following day.

The plan was to be executed on twentieth January. However, the night before the planned attack, government soldiers launched a fierce attack and killed scores of rebels, leaving many injured and scattered. The rebels had been taken unawares when the government forces attacked in the moonless night. Everyone had been sleeping and were woken up by missiles from the choppers that had been hovering over the camp. Though they eventually managed to shoot down the two helicopters; ninety rebels died that night, a hundred sustained injuries, and about five hundred escaped from the camp, scattering in all directions.

The bombs had hit two of Kayibanda's women's tents and four were dead, together with their children. This angered Kayibanda a great deal and at night he commanded his rebels to plan for an all-out war against Okot's government with immediate effect.

By noon the following day, the rebels had captured the main barracks and the government soldiers had joined the rebels. The government's army closed all the roads into the city but the rebels had already taken up positions and outnumbered them. By four in the evening, the city was singing with sounds of guns. Okot bundled all his family into a presidential jet and flew out of the country when many of his soldiers began defecting. Many of his ministers and senior security officers followed suit.

After Okot had been ousted by the National Army rebels, the rebel group established by Kayibanda, the whole country got entangled in a frenzy of celebrations. The rebels were triumphantly welcomed into the city centre as heroes because of what they had fronted as the reason for fighting the Okot government. The rebellion had lasted over five years. Kayibanda sat down with his senior men, one hundred in number now, and planned how to run the country. They agreed that the military government would lead for five years and later hand over power to civilians after elections. Kayibanda stood up and fiercely banged the table with his fists. He protested that five years was too long and instead suggested that they should lead for only three years and organise elections. The following day, Kayibanda was sworn in as president of Kalenga. He arrived at parliament in a gleaming blue Mercedes Benz wearing jungle green military fatigues and polished combat boots. His speech after the swearing in as president was captured thus:

'This is not a mere change of guards but a fundamental change in the politics of our country. Any individual or group who threatens the security of our people must be smashed without mercy. The people of Kalenga should only die of natural causes which are not under control but not from fellow human beings. The problem of Kalenga and Africa at large is presidents who overstay in power and those who rig votes and suffocate opposition. For us we are liberators and we shall liberate you from poverty, corruption, insecurity and all the biting problems.'

Kayibanda received thunderous applause and ululations after the impressive speech.

After assuming the office of president, Kayibanda appointed the senior men he had been with in the bush to different ministries and institutions. He awarded each of them a house in the posh suburbs of the city and all the properties which had been left behind by Okot and his supporters and cronies. The country was now peaceful and the people were hopeful that Kayibanda and his government would transform the country into something better in the shortest time possible.

Kayibanda had been in a relationship with Bamwine's daughter, Kabandize. He used to sneak out of the war zone and meet her outside the country where she had been studying. The duo had met when Kayibanda was at Heathrow Airport in London and they were happy to meet again. They had talked a lot about life and the politics of the country. She had also helped in mobilising financial support for the rebels during the bush war.

Kayibanda was now undecided about whom to marry between Kabandize and Kembaga. When Kayibanda moved into State House, he immediately moved in his entire family who had lived in Europe for quite long. However, he took his time to appear with Kembaga in any public gathering. His relationship status remained unknown. He bought properties for the innumerable women he had had fun with in the bush and appointed someone to look after each of them so that they did not cause trouble. He made arrangements with Kabandize, too, to fly into the country so that she could take him to her parents to discuss their planned marriage.

On the fifteenth, Kayibanda and Kabandize drove in a convoy of five vehicles to Chief Bamwine's home in Biguri. The chief was surprised to see his lovely daughter in the company of Kayibanda. He hadn't known that his daughter had come back to Kalenga – she had not communicated her arrival. Still, the chief was more surprised to see the president in his compound and wondered what had brought him after all the afflictions he had previously visited on him. He welcomed the president into the house, where his wife joined them and greeted the president and her daughter.

Kabandize was already in the kitchen preparing lunch. Now the president and Chief Bamwine talked at length, ranging from life in the bush to how Kayibanda was going to be different from the past leaders. When lunch had been served and the plates cleared away, Kayibanda thanked Bamwine and his household for their generosity.

"Another thing that brought me here, Mzee... I have come to ask for your daughter's hand in marriage. I want to marry your daughter Kabandize," he broached the subject. "She has told me several times to first come here and ask for permission from you but I have been busy in the bush fighting to liberate the country and end tyranny. Now I am here, not as a president but a suitor to your daughter. I would be happy if my request was taken into consideration, Mzee. Thank you."

Kayibanda then sat down, and swept his eyes around the living room where Chief Bamwine, his wife, Kabandize and her brothers sat. The speech had been short and precise. He had spoken with authority as though he was sure that Mzee would be thrown into a panic and hand over his lovely daughter.

Mzee Bamwine looked shocked at Kayibanda's presumptuousness. He expected him to first apologise for his past mistakes, dishonesty, and all the misconduct. But he was very boastful and disrespectful, and at the same time authoritative. Bamwine was not ready to kowtow to Kayibanda's disrespectful utterances despite the fact that he was now president.

Chief Bamwine cleared his throat and spoke with a strong voice. "Kayibanda," he started, "I took you to be my son when your father brought and dumped you here. At first, you proved to be a good boy. But then you started stealing my chickens and food and selling them without shame and consideration. I kept quiet. Then I took you to boarding school and hoped you would perhaps change. All was in vain. Still I didn't give up on you. You brought shame on my household when, several times, you raped other people's girls, but still I forgave you. But when you thought you did not need me anymore, you kicked me in the stomach. When you were a crime preventer, you unleashed terror on my supporters. And when we had won by defiance, you commanded your hooligans to steal my cows, around two hundred head, some of which were your father's. Still I forgave you. Later on, you brought your father and mother here and I welcomed you and helped him to settle down again. From then, this is the first time I'm seeing you. And you have the cheek to ask for my daughter's hand in marriage? What sort of person are you? For all the pain and humiliation you inflicted on me despite the priceless things I have done for you, you have never apologised. Now listen. If my beloved daughter wants to move in with you, let her do so on her own accord. Personally, though, I wouldn't want to see that happen. I have forgiven you your criminality and rascality, but, please, never dare use your authority as a president to torment me. I will curse you and you will die a miserable wanderer. You may now leave my compound."

Bamwine's speech was like a stab into Kayibanda's tummy. Everyone was shocked at such blunt words directed at the president. Kayibanda stood up, marched out of the house and jumped into a jeep. It sped off and disappeared in the dust towards his father's home.

Kayibanda found his father lonely and miserable. He had divorced Bekunda and now was living alone in poverty and squalor. The conditions in which Kayibanda found Kagurutsi were despicable and unbearable. The old man now had jiggers burrowing in his feet and hands. Kagurutsi had not even got to know yet that his son was president now. Bekunda had run mad and couldn't be traced anywhere. Kayibanda directed that a house be immediately constructed for his father, and some soldiers were dispatched to comb everywhere and find Bekunda. Kayibanda travelled back to the capital city in a jeep with his driver and without any escort vehicle. Kayibanda was now furious at Bamwine and his lack of respect for the president. He vowed to immediately take revenge.

Kayibanda had now been president for two years. He was busy enjoying the privileges of being a president. Within those years he had managed to discipline the army and the police, to disarm some cattle rustlers and subdue those who had rebelled against his government. But he had his trusted secretly trained assassins, twenty in number, who were ready to finish off his adversaries. None of his senior army officers knew about this secret arrangement apart from his brother Kanyeigabo, who was also a general. He sat down with his senior army and police officers, whom he had elevated to the rank of general, to plan for the country.

It was agreed in the meeting that all the political parties be banned and the country be a one-party state. It was also agreed that the country needed a constitution and delegates were chosen to work on it very quickly. Kayibanda made sure that the new constitution suited his prospects. He knew that elections were to be held soon and Okot would come back to the country and take part. So he smuggled an age limit clause into the constitution to block Okot, who was already over seventy-five years old. He also influenced the delegates to design a constitution that gave the president executive powers over everything and everyone in the country. The constitution gave him much of the powers he desired except the power to defy death and sickness. That one he didn't worry about because he was equipped with Bachwezi spiritual powers. In the same meeting, Kayibanda protested that the three years they had agreed to serve before handing over power to civilians in an open election was too short. He suggested that seven years be added to the three. It was also agreed in the meeting that a zero be added to the currency. Those who had one hundred shillings meant that they would get one thousand and those who had ten million would get one hundred million. He argued that this would strengthen purchasing power. It was later found out that he did it to enrich himself and his men instead.

During the meeting, five senior officers had openly disagreed with everything Kayibanda had proposed and he had marked them. After the meeting, he contacted his secret assassins and the five officers were eliminated before they could air their disagreements publicly. Those who had disagreed but kept their mouths shut were spared. This was contrary to what he had come into the presidency preaching. He had already started desecrating the mighty speech he had made on the steps of parliament after being sworn in as president. He had come to power espousing frugality but now he had started living luxuriously at the expense of poor Kalengans.

Kembaga was both of little school and ignorant. She lacked all the qualities to be the first lady of a country, but Kayibanda loved her very much. He was now stuck regarding what to do next.

Kembaga couldn't even express herself in English or any other language to address the nation. It took four years of training her in the English language and communication skills before she appeared in public to address the nation. Meanwhile, Kayibanda had never gone back to Kembaga's home to pay bride wealth. He had gone there only once when he was an assassin of president Ongoi and he had been told to bring forty cows. Kamagoba's parents, together with Tanyan authorities, had given up the search for Kamagoba. It was Kayibanda's secret and he vowed to die with it.

Kayibanda, who had expressed revulsion at corruption when he had just captured power, was one of the most corrupt presidents in the whole world. When members of his family or senior officers got involved in corruption, he would cover up for them. On the other hand, other corrupt civil servants would not be spared. Many national assets were sold off in his first four years at the helm and the buyers were only his family members and close associates. He had found a country which was the main exporter of agricultural products, but soon he destroyed cooperatives in order to uplift his tribesmen who mainly produced dairy products.

Kayibanda was still hurt that Chief Bamwine had embarrassed him. He retaliated by hiring some goons to grab and fence off fifty square miles of Bamwine's land. All the efforts the chief made to reach Kayibanda were futile. He died grumbling and stated in his will that Kayibanda, the alleged son of Kagurutsi, should not be allowed near his dead body.

Kayibanda had emerged from the bush looking emaciated. Even his veins could be seen through the skin on the temples, hands and legs. Now, after only three years in State House, he sported a potbelly and chubby cheeks. He surely couldn't see his feet or his erect penis when standing straight and looking down. He became shapeless; what with his huge stomach, flat buttocks, and small legs. He resorted to wearing free size shirts and a big hat with a wide brim to cover his huge cheeks all the time. He could now afford an opulent lifestyle from the huge budget allocated to State House, the budget which was four times bigger than that of health, agriculture and education combined.

Kayibanda's greed was insatiable. He continued to steal public properties and taxpayers' money with impunity. He, his family and relatives were the biggest importers of duty free goods in Kalenga. Their companies were exempt from tax and they would import large numbers of cars, spare parts, sugar, rice, phones, electrical appliances and what have you.

When Kayibanda ousted president Okot and installed himself as president, oil reserves had been discovered in the country and Okot had plans to have the oil drilled and sold to supplement government revenues. Kayibanda quickly got loans from the Global Bank to quench his thirst for money and used the undrilled oil as collateral security. He kept on promising the country that he would drill the oil and soon the country would jump into first-world status. However, the populace waited in vain, until they learnt about the huge debts that Kalenga was trapped in. Everyone would have to shoulder the burden of paying the debts until they died. Kayibanda had mortgaged the country for his own benefit.

When the time for elections came, his key competitors were harassed and imprisoned. Their supporters were beaten and imprisoned, too, and some of them were abducted and never seen again. Kayibanda had started showing his true colours. His dictatorial tendencies, greed for power and fear of competition were now very much in evidence. Though, on taking power, he had promised to organise elections in which neither he nor his fellow army officers, but only civilians, would take part, his name was to appear at the top of the ballot paper.

Later, two of his top army officers deserted and started a rebel group to fight against him. Kayibanda knew that many people's problem was money and that once given money they would shut up their voluble mouths. He directed the governor, Bank of Kalenga, to print more money, which was then stuffed into one hundred sacks. He hired a go-between, who visited the rebels in the bush and dished out the money to them. Allegiances changed quickly. The few who refused the money stayed put in the bush with the hope of ousting the thief in State House masquerading as a liberator of the people.

Kayibanda was surprised that a human being could actually refuse money. He decided to use blackmail against the rebels who had vowed to oust him. He realised that their justifications for the war were genuine and would sooner or later attract people's attention. Kayibanda would order his gang of assassins to attack villages close to where the rebels were active and cut off women's breasts and lips, and sometimes lock their lips with padlocks, rape children and kill men. Then he would use the atrocities committed by his own men to blackmail the rebels.

Kayibanda was a man who blamed everyone for everything and credited himself for every successful venture. He visited the area himself and promised the villagers that he would crush the rebels. When the international community turned their attention to Kalenga for crimes against humanity, the rebels denied having committed any such crimes and accused the government of blackmail. Kayibanda received huge amounts of money to fight the rebels but he pocketed much of it, using it to enrich himself instead. He would send his goons to attack villages and displace people and blackmail the rebels, then he would pretend to be collecting refugees and travel around the whole world holding out a begging bowl. When the international community became sympathetic and huge sums of money were released to help the situation, Kayibanda saw it as an opportunity to make money for himself. Kayibanda started destabilising other countries through warmongering, then he would collect refugees from those countries and cry out to the World Refugee Council for financial help. Kayibanda collected a lot of refugees, close to five million, settled them in camps and started making money. During the next elections, he registered all the refugees as voters and threatened to kill them or send them back to their home countries if they didn't vote him. Kayibanda won 80 percent of the votes. Everyone wondered how he had won the elections.

Rwehakanuzire, just like his sisters, was a thick-witted young man. He discontinued his journey to intellectualism when his A-level results came and he realised that he did not qualify for university. He was the only son of Kayibanda and Kembaga's. The rest of the children were girls who had also failed in school and dropped out. They had ended up managing their parents' businesses up to the time they got married.

Rwehakanuzire loved luxury and spent most of his time on beaches, travelling the world in his father's private jet, and splurging on women. Kayibanda could have influenced any university to admit his son but the son wasn't interested in continuing his education. After all, his father was a president and they had everything. He saw no reason to continue with school and train for a profession.

Kayibanda decided to take Rwehakanuzire to a military academy in America. Rwehakanuzire spent two years in intensive training. When he came back, he was again taken to Russia for another two years. He also underwent sword fighting training in the United Kingdom and when he returned to Kalenga he was immediately appointed as commander of the presidential guard. Then he started receiving promotions each year at the expense of those who had joined the army many years earlier.

After Rwehakanuzire had appeared on national television a number of times for demystification, he fell in love with the programme host, Wambu. She was a very beautiful woman. When she was approached by the First Son, she didn't see any reason to reject him since he was a young, handsome soldier with a bright future. They shared contacts and agreed to meet the following day at one of the five-star hotels in the city. Rwehakanuzire was in his early thirties and ready to marry Wambu. She was not from his tribe but he saw no problem with it.

When Rwehakanuzire told his parents about his marriage plans, his father was positive and happy for his son. However, Kembaga wasn't happy since she wanted his son to marry someone of his own tribe. His sisters, too, were opposed to the prospect of Wambu the journalist getting married to their brother since she had appeared in the newspapers in bikinis several times at different beaches with different men.

"You want to marry that Wambu prostitute who works at STV? That is stooping low. You are the son of the president and there are very many respectable women to marry in this country," Nyamwezi protested and walked out of the family meeting. Soon, the sisters followed suit.

Rwehakanuzire was now in the sitting room with only his parents. He looked on, taciturn. The room was devoid of noise until Kayibanda cleared his throat and ordered his daughters to return and sit down.

"Now listen to me. I am the head of this family and this is my son. He is grown up and, therefore, autonomous. He didn't come here to ask for permission to marry but to communicate that he is going to marry. If he wanted to, he would not tell us, because he has everything now. He has come here to tell us because he loves and respects us. All of you should stop being stupid. You are also ripe for marriage. Shall we choose husbands for you? Whoever is against the idea of my son marrying the woman he loves should march out of this home and never come back," Kayibanda said furiously and demanded a glass of water. "I want all of you to kneel down and apologise to him now. He is my only son and my heir so you need to respect him and his decision because he is a mature person." He gulped down a glass of water.

Rwehakanuzire felt feathers growing on his ribs. His father had never defended him like this before. He felt big, too, when all of his sisters knelt down and apologised, and when his mother followed suit and said sorry while shedding tears.

On the day they had met at the hotel, they had talked about themselves the whole evening over expensive food and drinks. Rwehakanuzire had sat opposite Wambu and when darkness started settling, he had shifted to where she sat and attempted to kiss her. She protested and suggested they should kiss on the second date. He offered her a wad of money as transport back home but she refused it. He offered to drop her off where she lived and, again, she refused. When Rwehakanuzire was being driven back home, he wondered at a woman who refuses a kiss from the First Son as well as money. At the same time, however, he thought that perhaps she was not lustful and a gold digger like the other women he had met before.

When Wambu reached home, she freshened herself and jumped on a boda boda to her boyfriend's apartment. She found the boyfriend, Baguma, in the kitchen cooking supper for himself and sat on the chair in the scullery and watched. Baguma wondered why she had not helped now as usual, and why she was moody.

"Hey love, are you sick? You are not the usual Wambu I know... what is the problem?" Baguma enquired while scooping the egg from the pan onto the plate without looking at her.

"Nothing. I have just come here to share with you something very urgent and I request your attention." Wambu sounded dead serious and Baguma found this scary. "If you want to listen to me, let's talk in the sitting room because the smell of your fried eggs is causing nausea in me," she added and moved away.

"My love, are you pregnant? I am ready to marry you if you

are. I cannot reject you my dear love," Baguma said as he sat next to her on the couch.

At the mere mention of pregnancy, Wambu realised that the days had elapsed and she had not had her period yet. It scared her, but she remained stoical.

"We are ending the relationship right now. I am no longer interested in you and that is what I am here to tell you. I never wanted to tell you on the phone. Please understand me and take it easy," Wambu said and got up to go.

There was a knock on the door. Bagaya didn't wait to be told to enter and she pushed the door open. To her surprise, she found Baguma holding Wambu's hand and pulling her back to the couch. Bagaya was Baguma's other girlfriend and when he saw her, he knew that his fate was sealed. He had played them for three years and had decided that he would settle down with whoever got pregnant first.

"I have caught you red-handed," Bagaya said, her voice chilly. "Tell me, who the hell is this and why is she here? I am here to tell you that I am pregnant by you and here you have been sneaking around with another woman behind my back!"

Bagaya marched towards where Baguma sat. He had let go of Wambu's hand and she stood there looking confused.

Wambu didn't wait for the drama to unfold. She found her way out of the house through the open door, stopped a boda boda and disappeared into the darkness.

Wambu cried the whole night and her pillow got drenched in tears. She wasn't crying because she was leaving Baguma but because she had been played all along. She had also missed her periods. She was carrying Baguma's baby yet she had just met the right man, Rwehakanuzire, son of the president. She shuddered at the thought of abortion because she had lost three of her sisters to abortion. She hatched a plan to visit her new boyfriend at his apartment and sleep there. He would not deny that the pregnancy was his since her tummy still looked normal.

The following day, when she had picked up the phone and started scrolling in search of his number, she saw on the screen a message reading:

"Hello darling, how was your night? Today after work please I am sending you a driver to pick you up. Please be ready by five in the evening. Love you and please take care."

Wambu couldn't believe what she saw. She was very happy. The hours she spent waiting up to evening were like months. After reading the evening news, she signed out. The first son's Range Rover Sport was already in the parking lot of STV waiting alongside a police lead car. She was surprised when soldiers saluted and opened for her the car door and it sped off through the jam following the lead car with sirens blaring. In fifteen minutes they were entering State House. She even pinched herself to make sure that she was not dreaming.

"Surprise...!" the president, his wife and daughters said in unison as Rwehakanuzire went down on the lawn on one knee while holding a ring. Wambu was still alighting from the Range Rover Sport whose doors had been opened by the soldiers. She was indeed surprised and speechless. The smile of happiness lasted for a few seconds and then she shed tears of joy.

"Will you marry me, Wambu?" Rwehakanuzire said happily while looking into Wambu's eyes.

Others were cheering on and clapping hands, as cameras flashed. Wambu stretched out her hand and Rwehakanuzire put a ringer on the middle finger. He then rose up and gathered her into a hug.

Wambu was officially welcomed into the family. After pleasantries Rwehakanuzire and Wambu drove off to the apartment where he stayed. The proposal function was telecast live and took Wambu unawares. She smiled the whole evening. Baguma fainted when he saw the engagement party on television and was rushed to hospital.

Rwehakanuzire wedded Wambu the following month and the function was very colourful. Wambu's parents were given five hundred head of cattle as bride price and a mansion in one of the posh suburbs of the city.

Wambu was the only surviving child of Onyango and Nabwire. Others had died a few years back. Wambu was now stuck with Baguma's pregnancy and feared to bet with abortion whose outcome she would testify was deadly yet she was not ready to discuss it with anyone.

****

When Kayibanda was seventy-two years old and his wife Kembaga sixty-nine, he directed the Minister of Presidency and National Guidance to declare their birth dates national holidays and to order that their huge portraits be hung in all the cities and towns. All the television and radio stations were directed to give live coverage of the event. He further directed that those who threatened to oppose the move be arrested and detained until the event was done. The Inspector General of Police indeed commanded his officers to put under house arrest all the opposition figures, and those who were caught on the streets were bundled into police vans and driven away to detention centres. On the occasion, a lot of money was spent to ferry uninterested people from villages to the independence grounds where they would get money, a plate of rice and a bottle of soda on alighting from the buses in which they were brought. Very many buses were sent across the country to ferry villagers because the organisers feared that the event would flop within the capital city, Mpanga. This trick of hiring and ferrying crowds also worked for him during the campaigns for president. He would be having a campaign rally somewhere but travel with his supporters in buses to the venue to avoid the disappointment of rejection by the locals in the area or to avoid media speculation that he was unpopular.

Hundreds of medical interns, together with their seniors, were seen on the streets marching to parliament displaying placards reading “NO DRUGS IN THE HOSPITALS”, “NO CANCER MACHINE”, and “WE NEED SALARIES” as the birthday celebrations for the president and his wife went on. The police used tear gas to disperse the crowds in vain. Soon other youths joined the procession and military police started using live bullets and arresting whoever was found on the streets to avoid uncontrollable and irate demonstrators.

The following day, all the opposition leaders were still under house arrest and several activists under detention in police cells. The activists were brought to court and charged with treason, sentenced to the country’s maximum prison for ten years; while the opposition leaders were all arrested and detained in police cells for no particular reason. They would be arrested every day in the morning and taken to unknown places and brought back in the night and dropped off in their homes daily. This was a move by the regime to stop them from reaching the city centre and inciting violence.

One day, Kibaate, the leading opposition political figure, beat the twenty-four-hour watch and proceeded to the city centre early in the morning. The previous night, police had brought him to his house and seen him enter the gate. They had then surrounded the house the whole night. In the morning they had forced themselves through the gate into the house to arrest him in order to take him into detention as usual. To their chagrin, however, he wasn’t in the house. How he had escaped, no one knew, because his house was under watch twenty-four seven. When General Byensi, the commander in charge of Kibaate, found out that they had been beaten at their game, he reported to his boss at the central police station. He was given strict orders by radio call to search everywhere lest he got demoted.

Meanwhile Kibaate had reached the city centre. When the people noticed his presence in the city, thousands joined him in a walk to Freedom Square. By the time he reached the city centre he had been joined by more than thirty thousand people and the city was at a standstill. There was a traffic gridlock and no car could move. The police officers were taken unawares. All roads were blocked and they had nowhere to pass with their tanks and armoured vehicles. Meanwhile, Freedom Square was under siege by all types of military units.

When Kayibanda saw what was happening in the city on national television and the internet, he directed the Communication Commission boss to cut off all the television and radio stations that were giving live coverage of the demonstration. He further directed that the internet be blocked and all the international journalists be arrested and detained. Kayibanda commanded the police chief to use jets and helicopters to disperse the peaceful demonstrators with water cannon and teargas since the city was accessible. The air force successfully dispersed the thousands of unarmed peaceful demonstrators with the use of low-flying jets and helicopters that sprayed pepper and teargas. This method had never been used before. When the demonstrators were sprayed, their bodies itched and burned, and eventually they gave up.

Kibaate was arrested together with a few others and bundled into a helicopter. They were then flown to an island in the middle of the lake where they were tried and charged with treason and sentenced to five years in prison.

In prison, Kibaate felt that he was not safe. He was imprisoned alone. He didn't know where those he had been jointly charged with were. He went on a hunger strike demanding that others be imprisoned in the same cell with him. After three days, they were brought to his cell.

A few days later, when the warders took Kibaate and his fellow detainees for labour in the sugarcane plantation, they escaped through the thick plantation and disappeared. A week after their disappearance, they were heard on an international British radio talking ill of the despotic Kayibanda government and beseeching the world to cut off aid and impose sanctions on Kalenga. The British government threatened to cut off all aid and expel Kalenga's ambassador in Britain if Kayibanda didn't stop harassing the opposition.

Kayibanda felt the punch in the face. He asked Kibaate and his fellows to return home and resolve the issues plaguing the country at a round table. He knew that the British government would ask its European counterparts and eventually other countries in the world to withdraw support from Kalenga. He knew that he would not manage to survive since the country depended ninety-seven per cent on foreign aid. Through his cadre judges, Kayibanda decided to drop all the charges against Kibaate and his fellows and requested them to come back and sit with him in a round table discussion. Kibaate knew all of Kayibanda's tricks. He knew that once you met him and he looked into your eyes the Bachwezi spirits would proselytise you into kowtowing to his dictatorship.

Kibaate and his fellows left Britain and returned to Kalenga.

But he vowed not to meet Kayibanda and instead issued a document detailing all the atrocities the president had committed and the entire plan for a life presidency. Meanwhile, his fellows went to State House after a week to meet Kayibanda and he appointed them district commissioners. Kibaate felt betrayed by the people he thought were comrades in the struggle. He was not, however, discouraged from moving on. He was determined to keep exposing the despot until the whole world knew about his wiles.

The constitution demanded that an elected president must serve only two terms, but when Kayibanda was serving what was supposed to be his last term, he hatched a plan to change the constitution and remove term limits. Still, Kayibanda knew that many people's problem was money. When he had first captured power using the gun, the first thing he had done was to voraciously 'make' money.

This time around, he invited all the members of parliament and sat down with them. Again, he directed the bank governor to print money and stash it in sacks. Kayibanda reached an agreement with the members of parliament that they would change the constitution to remove term limits in exchange for five hundred million in cash each. Ninety per cent of the parliamentarians were very happy about the money and ten per cent refused and walked away in protest.

Kayibanda, who had come to power preaching that the problems of Africa are caused by leaders who overstay in power, had now served twenty years and still wanted more. Now that he had finished using parliament to remove term limits from the constitution, he was free to contest again and again until he reached the age limit of seventy-five years.

After the members of parliament had conspired to remove the term limit from the constitution, they received resistance and death threats from their constituencies. Some were even advised not to set foot in their villages again and they decided to permanently live in the city, for fear of a backlash from the angry voters. The honourable members of parliament beseeched Kayibanda to come to their rescue because whatever they had done was to favour him even though they had received millions each. Now the huge monies they had stowed away couldn't give them protection against the angry masses. The president authorised the army commander to allocate a lead vehicle with six escorts to each of the five hundred members of parliament. A lot of tax money was used to procure the vehicles while the hospitals had no drugs and teachers, and doctors earned scandalously low salaries.

The populace felt betrayed and Kayibanda was worried that they would surely go out on the streets to demonstrate against the act. The army and military police were deployed heavily in every city and town to create fear in those who were hatching a plan to demonstrate. All members of the opposition were put under twenty-four seven surveillance, and the police strongly warned those who were thinking of using social media to incite violence.

Kayibanda was a strategic planner. He knew that he would be needing parliament to pass his draconian laws all the time. What he did was to help very many members of his ruling party to contest and win elections through massive rigging. The police and the army would be deployed during elections to harass and imprison opposition supporters. Then the ruling party candidates would use the opportunity to rig massively and go to parliament. Only a quarter of the members of parliament from Kayibanda's party were genuinely voted into parliament and a third were smuggled into parliament to his yes men and women. He created very many constituencies to bolster his support in parliament. These would pass whatever law or amendment he wanted passed without consulting their constituents.

Kayibanda had the executive powers to appoint the judges, Inspector General of Police, the army commander, the chairman of the Electoral Commission and all other heads of institutions. He also had the power to fire them in case they disagreed with him. This weakened the institutions. Instead of serving the populace, the institutions served Kayibanda and his family interests. The institutions owed him allegiance since those who manned them were subservient to the appointing god, Kayibanda.

When Kayibanda learnt that he had plunged the country into poverty and the economy was unravelling at a high rate, he knew that his grip on power was at stake. This time, he started using slow-killing poison from Russia and North Korea to finish off his opponents. His generals started dying one after the other and greatly reduced in number. When they had just captured power, there were thirty-four generals; of these, only ten now remained. Every general suspected of plotting something would be poisoned.

Kayibanda learnt that his security was at stake. He recruited two thousand loyal youth from his party and flew them to Russia for training. They were trained in defence skills and the use of the latest military equipment. Out of the two thousand, only one thousand five hundred returned. They were assigned only to protect the president and members of his family. Rwehakanuzire his son was appointed their commander. These presidential guards were equipped with better arms and skills than the national army. Another group of youth, five thousand in number, were sent again to Russia for training and after two years they returned and joined the presidential guard. Now that his security was assured, he felt sure that he now had the freedom to plunder the country to the bones.

Kayibanda would receive international aid and use it to do his personal businesses. He would use the money meant for combating HIV/AIDS and malaria to buy himself a presidential jet. He used the jet as an ambulance to fly himself and members of his family to foreign countries to treat even small illnesses like headaches. Very many people died of disease and poverty yet the money that would transform the country was only splurged on his family and very few associates in the system. Illiteracy and poverty levels grew more and more. Unemployment levels reached ninety per cent and the populace resorted to spending days and nights in churches, while some resorted to crime and others to full-time begging on the streets. Kayibanda loved such a situation because he internally reasoned that a poor and ignorant populace is easy to govern whilst informed and rich people are difficult to govern. These poor ones would receive some handouts from the president and clap hands, and vote him again and again. After elections, they would perish and suffer in poverty again.

Kayibanda used money and job appointments to buy off weak members of the opposition. There was no need to poison these ones, because they neither had guns nor any influence on his army. He bought them off to keep an uninformed population that didn't know their rights and privileges in that state. The money that would be used to build roads, put medicine in the hospitals, build schools or provide other services ended up in pockets of the few. Kayibanda didn't care because his family and close associates educated their children and got treatment abroad.

Kayibanda was now lumbering under the weight of crimes against humanity, ranging from warmongering to massacre and genocide. He was seventy-four years old and the constitution barred him from running for president again. He thought about this. The charges for these crimes awaited his retirement, when he didn't have presidential immunity and the army to protect him. He hatched a plan to remove the age limit from the constitution using parliament. He knew the weakness with the parliamentarians so he authorised the governor of the central bank to print money again. This time, he was afraid because the opposition would appeal to the citizens to demonstrate on the streets. He hatched another plan through the prime minister to introduce a public order control bill in parliament and it was passed into law. This law stated that it was illegal for anyone or a group to demonstrate against the government and those who broke this law would be imprisoned for life or face the death penalty. With this draconian law, Kayibanda knew that he would manage the errant opposition members of parliament.

Money was dished out to ruling party members of parliament, with each walking away with a billion shillings. They were the majority in parliament and so it was very easy.

The four surviving generals included Kayibanda himself. Two of them were nearing retirement but Kayibanda was reluctant to promote others. Meanwhile, his son Rwehakanuzire had shot up through the ranks and it was rumoured that the rapid promotions were part of Kayibanda's plan, after killing the old three generals, to appoint his son a full general so that he would have full control of the army. One of his generals fled the country and disseminated the dossier that detailed Kayibanda's plan. The general was followed abroad and poisoned. He was found dead in his bed in the morning and the postmortem report indicated that he had drunk juice laced with Russian poison.

Before Kagurutsi died, he had called his son Kayibanda and handed to him all the Bachwezi powers he possessed. His mother Bekunda was never found after she had run mad. She could have wandered into the wilderness and lions could have had her for dinner. Now he had the powers to look into a person's eyes and change their conscience so that they would only sing his praises. He would call those he feared to kill, such as religious leaders, to State House and sit with them to dinner. Then, the following day, they would be everywhere uttering things only meant to praise the dictator. Regardless of Kembaga's education level, Kayibanda appointed her minister of education. This gave Kayibanda the opportunity to steal land belonging to schools in the city for his personal benefit. He stole a lot of land and set up shopping arcades and several other real estate properties. By the end of thirty years in power, almost all the buildings in Mpanga town and other cities across the country belonged to him and his family. All the lucrative businesses that got government contracts belonged to Kayibanda's daughters and son and some other close relatives. Kayibanda had become wealthy and topped the list of the world's richest presidents. The man whose father was unknown, whose mother had escaped from home after the gang rape, whose parents had greatly suffered until he became president, had started compensating himself for the years he spent in poverty and despair.

Kayibanda appointed heads of institutions basing on loyalty rather than experience and professionalism. Only those who proved their worth in bootlicking and helping to torment or abuse the opposition would be welcomed and given jobs regardless of whether they had the right kind of education or not as long as they were good propagandists for the rogue regime. Kayibanda divided the country into many districts so that his growing number of bootlickers could get absorbed in their administration. He did this without minding the costs. He as well thought that by turning every county into a district he would bring services closer to the people, but this idea didn't work out. A bunch of loyal political rejects, too, would be appointed as district commissioners and others ambassadors to represent Kalenga in other countries. Many of them didn't even have an iota of international relations and diplomacy training or experience. Many of the political rejects or loyal cadres were appointed presidential advisors, too. In total, Kayibanda had over four hundred advisors. Some of these had never met him; and those he met often, he would instead advise them on what to do. Kalenga had the largest number of members of parliament and cabinet ministers in the whole world, yet it was the poorest and depended on aid and handouts from foreign sympathisers.

When Kagurutsi was passing on his spiritual powers to

Kayibanda, he urged him never to use them selfishly but only to protect himself from danger. However, after seizing the spiritual powers, Kayibanda took himself to be god. He misused the powers to punish or eliminate those who disagreed with him. The powers then turned against him. When he had just started his thirty-second year in power, Kayibanda started rotting in the left arm and his scrotum developed small rashes resembling the skin of a jackfruit. He thought it was perhaps a minor and easily curable sickness and was flown out of the country for treatment. The doctors did not diagnose any sickness and yet his condition was getting worse. This worried him very much because even his bowels could no longer hold firmly for long and he needed to wear diapers all the time. He bought himself a mobile toilet van and soon his motorcade increased to forty-one vehicles. He decided to look for the most powerful witch doctor in the whole world, and it is he who revealed to him the truth about his rotting body and found him temporary treatment.

Kayibanda started shirking presidential responsibilities because of his health. To attend to the most important issues he would show up in thick jackets and hand gloves to hide his condition. Soon, members of his family started making money from those who sought to see him. They would solicit money from investors and promise to arrange an appointment for them with the president. Kanyeigabo and his wife were the biggest beneficiaries of the president's ill health. Soon the news leaked to the media that millions of dollars had been collected from different investors who sought an appointment with Kayibanda.

One morning, while Kayibanda was strolling around the grounds of State House, guarded by his soldiers at each corner,

Rwehakanuzire's vehicle pulled into the parking lot with screeching tyres. Rwehakanuzire leapt out and dashed towards where his father was. This alerted the presidential guards, who hastily came and shielded Kayibanda.

"Can I have a quick word with you? And now! In the boardroom!" Rwehazanuzire commanded his father.

Rwehakanuzire would have been killed if he wasn't Kayibanda's son. Also, he commanded the presidential guard, and that was why he was left to access the State House and the compound where the President had been jogging. Rwehakanuzire had picked up some information that Kembaga was not his mother and that his mother Kamagoba had disappeared mysteriously at the instigation of Kayibanda when they were still studying at university. He had been quite suspicious basing on the way Kembaga had been discriminating against him. Even the love that exists between mother and child - the love and attachment got from the mother's breast - was not there.

Kayibanda looked at his son, surprised. 'Is he under the influence of drugs, alcohol or spirits?' he asked himself. He ordered his son's immediate arrest and detention in one of the cottages at State House. The guards thought it humiliating arresting their commander, so they did not obey the order. They instead watched on as Rwehakanuzire marched into the house through the lawn. Kayibanda followed him quickly.

'WHO AND WHERE IS MY MOTHER? I WANT ANSWERS RIGHT NOW!' Rwehakanuzire screamed, pulled out his pistol and aimed at Kayibanda's bald head. All this happened in the corridor adjacent to the boardroom.

Kayibanda turned into a shadow and, at the speed of lightning, disarmed Rwehakanuzire, kicked him in the crotch and both disappeared into the wall like ghosts. Rwehakanuzire regained consciousness when they were both on a plane rumbling through space to a place he didn't know about. He had always treated with incredulity stories about his father and grandfather being Bachwezi but now he needed no further proof. Kayibanda had killed the guards on duty that day to avoid dissemination of what had happened between the president and his son. It ended there and then without a third party. He was now calm and composed. There were only two in the plane save for the pilot and the stewardess who served them food and drinks. Rwehakanuzire got up from his seat and walked across the aisle to join his father who was busy reading newspapers and soon they were absorbed in a conversation.

When they had come back from hibernation, Kayibanda promoted his son to the rank of full general and appointed him second commander of the armed forces. This meant that he deputised the president in giving commands to all the armed forces in the country. He met with his son and requested him to forward five names of his most loyal cadres to be promoted. Rwehakanuzire picked up some of his half-brothers whom Kayibanda had sired with different women while in the bush. Now the youthful generals were his own sons. By the time the other two generals learnt about the shocking news of exclusion from military affairs, the slow killing poison had weakened them and the shock catalysed their collapse. One died in a hotel room where he had gone to philander with a prostitute and another one died on the steering while driving. His car skidded off the road and hit a tree and burst into flames.

Kayibanda also announced a cabinet reshuffle where he named his wife Kembaga vice president. He did all this because his health was not getting any better and he was expecting to die any time. If he died, his wife would be president and his son commander-in-chief of the armed forces, according to Kalenga's constitution. The army officers who were suspected of plotting something against the rogue regime were immediately eliminated mysteriously without anyone suspected of having killed them. The few opposition figures were allowed to oppose the regime for the sake of portraying Kalenga as a democratic country. Otherwise Kalenga was a failed state in one man's hands. All the opposition did was talk in press conferences and write on social media but efforts to demonstrate on the streets or take up arms were foiled innumerable times. The few who took to the streets to demonstrate would be killed instantly, which created fears among the populace regarding future remonstration against the government. The main opposition political party, which was very popular, had won elections several times, only for the Electoral Commission to announce the incumbent winner at gun point.

At eighty-two years, Kayibanda had all the money, the army was in his hands and power, too, was concentrated in his family. His brother, Kanyeigabo, was now the Chief Justice. His first son-in-law was in charge of the Electoral Commission and Rwehakanuzire's wife the Prime Minister. His second son-in-law was the Inspector General of Police. Now he felt comfortable and had no stress deriving from the possibility that someone else was eying his seat.

At eighty-seven years, Kayibanda was pensioned off and wasn't able to walk anymore, so he had to be taken around in a wheelchair. It shocked everyone when he announced that he would run again for president. There was a lot of criticism coming from different corners of the world but he didn't heed it. Those who vowed to protest against the dotard's bid were threatened with violence. The leaders of all the opposition political parties were arrested and stopped from campaigning. Only Kayibanda the barbarian was left to campaign up to the end and, on Election Day, the opposition politicians were released so they could vote for themselves. Civil society organisations appealed in vain to the Electoral Commission to postpone the sham electoral process. The ruling party secretary general, who was often referred to as "big pig" because of her elephant-like fatness, appeared on national television and threatened that those who contested the outcome of the election results would be killed. When the results started coming through into the national tally centre, it was evident that Kibaate, the flag bearer of the biggest opposition party, would win the elections with a big margin. The results kept flowing in and Kibaate's results shot to eighty percent whilst Kayibanda's were still only at ten per cent and reducing. The Inspector General of Police and the army commander stormed the national tally centre and directed the Electoral Commission chairman to announce Kayibanda as winner of the elections. Meanwhile all the opposition leaders had been arrested, charged with treason and flown to a prison in the middle of the lake. All this took not more than one hour to happen. The votes had been rigged massively for the parliamentarians under the auspices of the partisan security forces. After the parliamentarians had been sworn in, they were gifted with bulletproof vehicles and large sums of money.

The economy deteriorated further and the value of the shilling plummeted. Inflation became uncontrollable and the prices of basic commodities escalated. Kayibanda and his family, together with their cronies, didn't feel the pinch, of course, because the money they had made was enough even for their offspring, even one thousand years henceforth. Kembaga appeared on national television and blamed parents who blamed the government for their poverty and their being hungry. She threatened to arrest all the parents who weren't able to pack food for their school-going children. This was a mockery to the poor majority. They had been made poor by the poor government policies and the national budget that served only government institutions but not the populace.

Kayibanda allocated all the swamps and parts of forests to pseudo-investors to set up factories. He argued that building factories in wetlands and forests was better than growing yams there. This was not surprising, though, since he was a simple goatherd who learnt how to speak and write English and hold a gun. Some Indians who had factories in Kalenga enjoyed tax holidays and cheap labour, they mistreated Kalengans and expatriated their profits to develop their own country. There was no investment policy at all to protect the local investors. Very many foreigners would get cheaper loans from their countries and come to Kalenga to start up small-scale retail businesses and sell their goods cheaply whilst the locals would suffer with high-interest loans and stiff competition with the foreigners.

Whereas other presidents would be launching new advanced means of irrigation, Kayibanda would be busy launching bottle irrigation methods where one is required to collect mineral water bottles and fill them with water and hang them on top of a young plant or place them under a mature plant. One wondered how one would be able to irrigate one's many acres of millet or maize this way. Other presidents would be launching the fortieth aircraft and new routes to Europe and America while Kalengans would be celebrating the anniversary since their airline and railways were sold off and the money shared by a few individuals.

When Kayibanda learnt that there was no longer a bush where people would go to rebel against him and that people were instead using social media to expose his rogue regime to the outside world, he introduced social media tax where everyone using mobile internet to access the internet would pay some money first. This angered the stoical and nonchalant populace the more. It was insensitive of Kayibanda to over-tax the populace through some commodities and again want to tax social media, yet the country's revenue ended up stowed into the pockets of the few. Kayibanda and his gang of criminals felt no shame in coming up with social media tax yet other countries provided free internet access to their populace.

Then, one day, the populace plucked up the courage to rebel against the Kayibanda government. They took to the streets and braved teargas and live bullets. On the first day of the defiance campaign against the rogue regime, nine hundred and seventy people were arrested, thirty killed and five hundred injured. This captured international attention and criticism of Kayibanda's government mounted. Threats were made to impose sanctions if security forces continued to kill unarmed people with impunity.

On the second day, thousands of people demonstrated on the streets of different cities, holding up placards demanding that

Kayibanda resigns. This time water cannons, teargas and bullets failed to disperse the demonstrators. The police and the military shot at the demonstrators in full view of the international media and soon the issue of Kalenga attracted international sympathy. The police cells were full to the brim of those arrested, the prisons too were full, and the police were stuck with those they had arrested. People kept thronging the streets in solidarity until they overpowered the security forces and confiscated their guns and teargas. When the police and the army realised that the revolt was unrelenting, they joined the protestors. Kayibanda, together with his still loyal bootlickers, were now entangled in shit. The protesters were now marching on State House. His presidential jet was shot down on the runaway as it gained speed to take off. His family and some associates perished in the plane when it burst into flames.

Poor Kayibanda had mistakenly thought that all he needed was money, power, soldiers and the spirits of Bachwezi to rule the people of Kalenga. When the populace realized that their votes didn't matter but that instead it was those who counted the votes who determined the winner, they got fed up and Kayibanda thought they were stupid. He could have chosen to be a dictator who worked for his country. Instead he was a selfish dictator who mainly worked for his family. Kayibanda had no real friends throughout his life. He treated everyone like diapers that he would use to fulfil his missions and discard. He was the kind of dictator who used people as ladders to reach where he wanted and then kicked the ladder and even burned it after landing. He was a professional philanderer who took advantage of women whom he offered appointments and other assignments. When Kayibanda was in the bush, he combed through the neighbouring villages and kidnaped teenage ladies who were not married and sneaked them into the camp. He had fun with them until he became president. He then rewarded them with properties and money on condition that they gave him his children. He appointed someone to take care of the children until they grew up and were absorbed into his praetorian guard.

A few weeks after Kayibanda, Kembaga, Rwehakanuzire and ten of his children had been killed in the presidential jet, the Speaker of Parliament called for the elections to choose a new president. All his cronies and relatives had escaped the wrath of the people's power by fleeing to the neighbouring countries, from where they connected to Europe and America. Some of the regime apologists, propagandists and members of parliament who thought that their security was not guaranteed fled the country and left their positions vacant.

Kibaate, who had been a thorn in Kayibanda's flesh for about four decades, won the elections overwhelmingly, hauling in ninety-seven per cent of the votes. He was sworn in and he promised to be the people's servant and a leader who would act on people's needs and problems. Kibaate, seventy years old, now president of Kalenga, started by appointing six judges to work on a new constitution that would be pro-people. He appointed his interim judges, Inspector General of Police, army commander, Prime Minister and Vice President and left other appointments to be made by the Vice President with the help of the Prime Minister and ministers. When the new constitution had been tabled in parliament for approval, it was found that it was the best constitution in the whole world and it was not tenable to amendments. The term and age limits had been brought back in, the powers of the president had been reduced and all the draconian laws Kayibanda had smuggled in were eliminated. Very many fellow presidents criticised him because of the constitution that was not tenable to amendments. Unsurprisingly, those who criticised Kibaate most strongly were those who had tightened their grip on power. Within three years, their governments were overthrown, one after the other, perhaps because the wind had blown from Kalenga towards other countries still ruled by dictators.

Kibaate appointed only competent people to his cabinet. Those who understood the workings of the ministries were to preside over them and ensure that what was required was done. He was a frugal man and promised to use his frugality to preside over a country of equal opportunities and shared prosperity. Parliamentarians and all other public officials were required to buy their own cars. The government only bought vehicles for the President, his vice, the Chief Justice, the army commander, the Inspector General of Police, the Speaker of Parliament, and the deputy Speaker of Parliament. Other civil servants and directors of different government authorities were required to use their own cars or request the government to buy them cars on the understanding that they would use their salaries to pay back the money with interest.

All the assets Kayibanda had acquired were nationalised except for his village home in Biguri. The budget now was stupendous and catered for priorities, not the comfort and luxury of those in power.

When Kibaate finished his first five-year term, he announced that he wouldn't take part in the next elections despite his immense popularity and everyone pleading with him to stay on. He respected the constitution which barred him from running for president again because of age. He had finished reorganising the country and setting up a good foundation for the next president. Kibaate led Kaleng for only five years but registered tremendous improvements in all the sectors. What he achieved in five years, Kayibanda didn't achieve in his reign of forty-three years. Kayibanda's rule was mainly about looting and self-enrichment. Foreign researchers and analysts wrote widely in foreign newspapers opining that if Kibaate remained president for another fifteen years, Kalenga would be the first African country to attain first-world status.

THE END.

Milton Keynes UK
Ingram Content Group UK Ltd.
UKHW021341020424
440487UK00009B/806

9 783982 513201